To Janis

Titles in this v

C000021722

Dementia Adventure (At Blackwaterfoot)

Seaweed In Her Hair

Best Wishes

Nick Cornwall

DEMENTIA ADVENTURE (AT BLACKWATERFOOT)

MILLER CALDWEL

Published by

Scotland
www.beul-aithris-publishing.com

First published 2021

©Miller Caldwell

ISBN 9798457916258

ABOUT THE AUTHOR

Miller Caldwell is a Scottish-based writer of novels.

He graduated from London University, having studied African industrial development, traditional African religions, and the colonial history of West Africa. He has had articles published in health magazines and *The Scottish Review*.

Following a life of humanitarian work in Ghana, Pakistan, and Scotland, he has gained remarkable insights into human nature. He brought an African president to tears in West Africa in 2002, and he confronted Osama bin Laden near Abbottabad, in the NWFP of the Islamic State of Pakistan in 2006. He was, for ten years, the local chair of the Scottish Association for the Study of Offending. He also served on the committee of the Society of Authors in Scotland as its events manager.

Miller plays a variety of brass, woodwind, and keyboard instruments, which provide a break from writing. Married, he has two daughters and lives in Dumfries, in southwest Scotland.

Dedicated to all authors with disabilities or chronic illness.

1

Ronnie Jackson's 12-foot wooden clinker rowing boat and his Ford Capri car were sold on his doctor's orders. To most people that would create a seismic change of lifestyle but for Ronnie, his mild cognitive impairment had slipped, and he was now officially diagnosed in the moderate category of dementia. He took his sudden recreational and medical restrictions in his stride.

Life had its limitations for him now, of course. But familiarity and regularity enabled him to get up each morning, make a substantial breakfast, dress and get outside. The great out-of-doors meant beach walks at Blackwaterfoot on Arran where he lived and had lived all his life. He seemed to know every grain of sand. When questioned why he never married, he told enquirers that in Blackwaterfoot he had never found the right woman. In truth, since his parents died some twenty years ago, he was happiest in his own company. Although he had been the local postman, a most solitary profession, he knew everyone in the small west Arran coastal village and further beyond. His former work required an early start to the day. His retirement did not alter that daily routine; that pattern was established and he rose very early each morning.

One such April day, Ronnie began his walk along the golden beach. The minimal light at that early hour cast its pale glaze over the sea as the wind whipped up the white wave caps transforming them into a fine spray. Ronnie took a deep breath and closed his eyes for a moment. That was one of a few of his daily routines too. However, this time when his eyes opened, his gaze was attracted to something in the water. He rubbed them to rid encrusted sleep from his eyelashes. He stood still. His focus was now fixed on a light in the dark water. Not a strong beam but one intermittently disappearing from time to time, as the waves danced around it. Yet it was not fading. It grew larger by the moment, in fact.

Ronnie squatted behind a turf of seagrass to observe, to make sense of what was happening. He watched the craft eventually make shore and a man jumped out with two bags. He ran quickly out of sight into the village. Then in no more than a few moments, he returned empty-handed to the boat which the skipper had turned around to make a quick departure. As the boat set off again down the east coast of Arran, and out of sight, a muddled mind made sense of what had happened.

Back at his home, as his mantelpiece dark mahogany clock struck 9 am, he lifted the telephone and dialled 01786 289070.

Sergeant Rory Murdoch received the call at Lamlash police station. He nudged his favourite Guatemalan coffee along his desk to pick up the phone. He knew the caller.

'Hi, Ronnie. So, you think it's a drugs run?' Rory asked swallowing his second mouthful of coffee.

'Definitely. You need MI5 up here, the taser-squad, the forensic people, the police helicopter.... you know?' Ronnie said crisply.

Sergeant Rory Murdoch sighed. 'Steady on my friend. A drugs drop at Blackwaterfoot? That's highly improbable. Not economically viable I'd say.'

'I think you should investigate before someone gets killed.'

Rory gulped his next mouthful. 'And... who is likely to get killed, Ronnie?' the sergeant asked inquisitively.

There was a hesitation. Rory inclined his ear.

'You still there, Ronnie?'

'I'm thinking....there's always someone who gets killed.'

A broad grin suddenly took hold of Rory's face. 'I think you have been watching too many cop dramas.'

'Cop dramas? Well, some....but they are bringing the drugs by sea, I tell you. You should get over here with a squad of armed detectives.'

'Listen, Ronnie, I'll get over to see you some time. Now don't you get yourself worried, will you promise me? The matter is in police hands now.'

Ronnie smiled. His message had got through.

A little over a week later Ronnie was again patrolling the beach before daybreak. Once more he spotted a boat near the shore. The same thing happened. The skipper stayed on board while the other man ran up the shoreline and two minutes later, returned empty-handed. It was time to inform Sergeant Rory Murdoch of his observations, once more.

'Well Ronnie what's it this time?' asked Rory stirring his usual Guatemalan coffee round and round in his cafetière, as he held the phone in his other hand.

'Same again,' he said. 'A drug drop and then off down the coast. It's a quick operation. You'll need the flying squad,' said a perturbed and excited Ronnie.

Rory drummed his pen on his office desk. 'I think I'd better come and see you, Ronnie. When will it be convenient?'

'It would have to be in the afternoon after I have done my postal round.'

Rory scratched his head. 'But you are no longer the postman. That's now Ethel McGinnis, isn't it? She took over from you about six years ago. You've got some real memory issues, haven't you Ronnie?'

'Then I'll be at home,' was all Ronnie could say.

At four pm that afternoon the blue and yellow diced police car marked Poileas Alba to appease Gaelic speakers and introduce the language to the majority arrived outside Ronnie's home. Rory got out, placed his chequered hat on his head, and knocked on Ronnie's door.

Ronnie answered the door and acknowledged Rory. 'What can I do for you today, sergeant?'

'Well, perhaps I can come in and we'll sort this out,' the sergeant said stepping forward.

Rory entered Ronnie's bungalow and saw the mess it was in. He pointed. 'Let me sit here if I take the jumpers off the seat.' Rory was used to disarranged lounges in the course of his police work.

'Yes, that's a good place to sit,' Ronnie agreed.

'Do you get any help, to support you living here?' Rory asked with a puzzled look as he looked around the dishevelled room.

'Help? No. I don't need help. If I need help, I call you,' the confused words fell from his lips.

Rory nodded with a lip-curving smile. Best to keep him onside, he thought. Back to business and get this over. He took out his notepad and began to record the interview.

'So, when do you see the drug drop?' the sergeant asked.

'In the mornings, I've seen them. I see them when I go out to work.'

Rory hesitated, lifted his pen, and smiled.

'And at what time is that?'

'I get up early. I have to start work early, you know, so I get up. I think it's about a quarter to 4 when I leave my house. Yes, about then.'

'But Ronnie you are no longer working, you should lie in bed till later,' said Rory almost sternly.

'Am I not allowed to get up early?' he asked like an errant schoolboy.

Rory grinned. He wondered how to reply for a moment. 'Your body needs rest. You get up when you want, but you don't need to get up as early, now you are retired.'

'So how would you know about the drug drop if I didn't see it at 4 am?'

Rory could not hide a more smiling grin. It seemed a catch 22 situation for him, so he relied on his police training.

'So, tell me what were the men wearing? Can you give me a description of them?'

Ronnie's head looked at the ceiling. He shook his head. 'It was dark. I could not see them very well.'

'Just keep that thought there. What size were the men, tall, medium, small, bearded, white, what were they wearing?'

'Too many questions,' he replied anxiously wringing his hands, with distress etched on his face.

'Okay, height?'

After a moment, Ronnie relaxed. 'The one on the boat, the skipper, I could not say, I only saw half of him. The man who ran up the beach with the bags was thin, I think. Not fat anyway.'

'Good and what did he wear?'

'Dark clothes. A dark top and dark jeans.... oh....and white socks. Yes, I remember now, white socks.'

'Was he wearing white socks on the first time or the second time he ran up the beach?' Rory asked taking Ronnie seriously, for a moment.

'Well, it was.... on the....um...I don't really remember.'

It was a false start. Rory closed his notebook. 'Blackwaterfoot is not a den of iniquity. There's not a drug problem in the village, you hear me?' he asked staring into Ronnie's eyes.

'Ah, you see. No drugs in town. That's where the dealers go. It's the start of something big, I tell you.'

Rory smiled and nodded to appease Ronnie as he replaced his notebook in his pocket.

'If I don't get any more evidence, I'll have to put your complaint to one side, you realise. I have more important things to do.'

'But if I see them bringing drugs to the shore, I must report them,' said an outraged Ronnie raising his voice.

Rory counted to ten in silence. Some home truths were required. 'What I am really saying Ronnie, is that I'll have to charge you with wasting police time if there is no crime. I don't want to do that but that's the consequence of finding no evidence because there's none there. I can't come out to see you every time.'

There was a silence. Ronnie took the solemnity of the moment seriously. Rory was pleased his words seemed to be sinking in.

But Ronnie's mind was elsewhere. 'You want a coffee?'

'Not today, Ronnie. I have work to do. Another time perhaps?' he suggested to appease his informer.

'Yes, another time,' Ronnie laughed. Suddenly a sad face appeared. 'I think I don't have any coffee anyway,' he smiled inanely.

2

Ronnie watched the long-tailed tits feed at his peanut feeder stand in the back garden while also drying dishes when the front doorbell rang. He dried his hands. He treaded through the messy lounge to the front door and opened it.

'Hello, Ronnie, my name is Ann, Ann Collins. I am a home help adviser,' she informed him as her initial assessment of her client began.

'That's good. You must do a lot of good work,' Ronnie responded with a long smile.

'That's what I want to speak to you about.'

'To me?' asked Ronnie in total surprise.

'Yes, I think you need some help,' she suggested.

'Help?' Ronnie repeated as Ann stepped forward into his home.

Ann was allowed into his lounge where she revealed it was a call from the police to social services which brought her to his home. Ronnie tried as he might to make the connection but failed.

'I know you have dementia, so we want to help you to stay in your home, as long as possible.'

'I can stay in my home. That's where I live.'

Ann nodded and smiled at him. 'Of course. What I feel would be good for you is to have a lady visit you to keep the rooms tidy, perhaps help you to shop, perhaps do your washing, that sort of thing.'

Ronnie hesitated. 'I don't need a wife. Thank you.'

Ann laughed as Ronny scowled. He had not seen the humour of his own remark.

'The lady I have in mind is a married lady. She will help you to adjust to your needs around the house. Her husband could help with your garden too if you like.'

'I see,' said Ronnie thinking that might be a good idea, yes, help around the garden.

'So, would you be happy with this arrangement?'

'I think so.'

'I should tell you; your home help comes from Romania. Her name is Elena. Her husband, Marius, works at the Kinloch hotel, as an odd job man.'

'But if she comes from Romania, she will arrive late. I may be out?' he asked with contorted eyebrows of concern.

'I'm sorry Ronnie, I just meant to say she comes from Romania, yes; but they live in Lagg now.'

Ronnie took a moment to reflect on what she had told him. 'But if she lives in Lagg, she does not come from Romania.'

Ann was perplexed. He was right, Elena came from Lagg so could not come from Romania.

'Yes, that's right. She's just down the road at Lagg,' she said to clarify his muddled mind.

Ronnie seemed distracted, turning his head towards the door.

'Elena can start on Monday morning if that suits you.'

'Monday, coming here? I had better tidy the house.'

Ann smiled and touched Ronnie's arm as she stood up to leave. 'No, don't you worry about the house. Elena will attend to that for you. You'll see.'

On Monday, Ronnie answered the door to a dark-haired woman in a sky-blue tunic with two outsized front pockets. She carried a bag over her shoulder.

'Yes, can I help you?' said the ever helpful and polite Ronnie.

'I'm Elena, your home help,' she said with an eastern European accent.

'I see,' he said without opening the door any wider.

'Did Ann not tell you I was coming on Monday morning?'

Ronnie screwed up his face then relaxed. 'Do you work with Ann?'

'Yes, she's my boss.'

'Then come in. She said you would be coming on Monday.'

'Yes, this is Monday.'

'Oh, is it?'

By 4 pm Elena had accomplished much. The lounge was presentable; washing was on the line; plates had been washed and replaced in the appropriate cupboards and the Hoover had travelled round all the rooms. She laid out his evening meal too. Just before she ended her first day's work, Ronnie followed her out to the garden as she gathered in his washing.

'You know there are drug smugglers in Blackwaterfoot?'

'Now, is that a fact?' she replied as she turned to look at him.

'I know it's a fact; the police don't.'

'I think the police will be monitoring the illegal activity. They won't talk about such operations, I suspect.'

'Oh, I see.'

'I am listening for when the spotter plane comes,' he replied turning to look heaven wards.

On Tuesday morning, up as early as usual, Ronnie set off for the beach once more. He looked over the water and the boat was fast approaching the shore once more. This time he had been seen. He stood still to see what would happen next. The boat turned sharply as if to abort the drug drop. That action sealed it in Ronnie's mind.

At 9 am later that morning Ronnie telephoned the police at Lamlash. Sergeant Murdoch took the call once more.

'Hello, Ronnie speaking. The drug runners went away this morning.'

'That's good to know Ronnie. Thanks for letting me know. Goodbye.'

The phone went dead. Ronnie's hand remained on the telephone cradle. Yes, he wanted to say more to the sergeant. Ronnie redialled.

'Yes?'

'I think they saw me, that's why they did not land. Then they set off without dropping off the drugs.'

'Okay Ronnie, I've got that. Now you get back to bed. Don't phone me unless it's urgent, you understand? Remember what I said, too many calls, and I'll have to charge you with wasting police time.'

'You mean you are not coming out to Blackwaterfoot? The village will soon be full of drugs,' he said raising his voice.

3

There was no drug activity that Wednesday morning but when Elena arrived, she brought her husband Mario who would tend to the garden.

Ronnie was not his usual self. He felt depressed. Rory Murdoch did not believe him and that hurt. The day had also started with a humongous downpour which left the flowerbeds bright but beaten. Marius got to work reviving them with canes. Ronnie went outside to see what he was doing. Mario's English was not as fluent as his wife's but he managed to be understood by Ronnie. It wasn't long before Ronnie told him of his concerns about drugs arriving in Blackwaterfoot.

'Where from the drugs?' asked the no-nonsense Mario.

'Where from the drugs?' he repeated as he thought through his reply. 'From a boat which drops the drugs by the Blackwaterfoot slipway. A man runs out with usually two bags and returns to the waiting boat. Its engine is quietly ticking over.'

Mario pouted his lips. 'How often have you seen this?'

'Several times,' said Ronnie pleased that someone was at last taking an interest in his discovery.

'At what time the boat come?'

'Very early in the morning.'

Mario pursed his lips. 'How early?'

'Now you ask, it's usually before 4 am,' Ronnie nodded.

'Why you up at that time? Can't you go sleep?'

'I always get up early. I am a postman.'

Mario clipped another dahlia to its cane. Then he looked up at Ronnie directly. 'So why doesn't the police do anything about it?'

'Good question. I think they don't believe me.'

Mario smiled.

The next morning when Elena was busy in Ronnie's home, dusting and window cleaning, Mario at home in Luss, telephoned the police at Lamlash.

'Hello officer, my name is Mario Balan from Luss. I wish to report crime.'

'I see and where has that crime taken place?' asked Rory.

'At Blackwaterfoot.'

His eyes opened wide. 'Don't tell me more drugs have been found?' Rory laughed.

'No, there is no drug problem at Blackwaterfoot at all, but there is one man they call Mr. Ronnie Jackson.'

'Oh yes, I know who you mean,' Rory sighed, placing his hand on his forehead.

'Well, he told me he be making up these stories about boats bringing drugs to Blackwaterfoot. The police should know about this. He is not living in the real world. He's not right in the head. You understand?'

'Making the stories up? You sure?'

'I not have tell you if it not be true,' said Mario in his improving English.

'I see. Thank you very much, Mr. Balan. Very interesting information indeed. Can you put your concern in writing and send it to me?'

'Yes, I try. My English written is not as gut as my speaking, but I try.'

At 9 am the following morning with speckled white striations in the sky above, Sergeant Murdoch and Constable Helen Dodds set off from their office in Lamlash. The sun was in their eyes but they made progress with heavy hearts. Ronnie was such a nice man; he had been a well-liked honest postman and now a sufferer of dementia but the law of the land must hold sway and hence their progress that morning.

Just over half an hour later they arrived at Ronnie's home. Helen knocked on the door and Ronnie answered it promptly with a smile.

'Ah, Sergeant and your friend do come in. I've got some coffee for you this time,' he said. The two officers entered and made their way into the spacious lounge.

'My, the lounge is very tidy, Ronnie. Not like last time I called,' he remarked.

'Elena cleans for me and helps me get things done.'

'I'm pleased to hear it,' said Helen.

'Ronnie, have a seat, please. This is an important visit. I'm afraid it not good news for you and I am the first one to say so.' He paused and took a deep breath.

Ronnie was aware of the serious look on the sergeant's face. Perhaps he was taking his sightings more seriously.

'Ronnie Jackson, you are charged with wasting police time on various dates over the last four weeks. You have the right to remain silent. Anything you say may be recorded and used in evidence in a court of law, do you understand?'

'Really, interesting,' he replied.

Rory put away his black notebook and stood up.

'You have to come with us back to Lamlash. We'll take you to Ayr on the afternoon sailing. Ayr Sheriff Court will sit the next morning. Ronnie, you'll need a lawyer.'

Ronnie was grateful to have a take-away serving of lasagne for a late lunch in the sparsely furnished detention cell at Lamlash. It was not locked.

Can I have something to drink?' he enquired as he appeared behind the charge desk.

'Certainly, I'll bring you a tumbler of water and a cup of tea shortly afterwards,' said Helen.

'Thank you very much,' said Ronnie with a generous smile and returned to his private office, as he understood the cell of his incarceration to be.

Later that afternoon Ronnie accompanied Rory on the boat to Ardrossan where, on arrival, they were met by two Ayr police officers.

'Hi Rory, is this the prisoner?' asked Constable Mike Mason as Constable Norrie Clark brought out the handcuffs.

'Yes, Ronnie Jackson, retired postman. Hey, you won't need these, Norrie. He's got dementia. He won't run.'

Ronnie's eyes flirted between the two unknown police officers. He had heard one of them had dementia. He thought it to be Norrie.

'Orders. Can't change them. You know that Rory,' Norrie said locking Ronnie's wrists together.

'Where am I going?' asked Ronnie concerned as this unfamiliar meeting progressed.

'To Ayr police station overnight,' said Mike Mason. 'It's to Ayr Sheriff Court tomorrow morning, you'll be going.'

Ronnie did not reply. He could make little sense of what was happening. He sat back in the police car as it winded its way up the west coast to Ayr. When asked if he was comfortable, he did not answer. He was descending into a pit of depression once more. He had no control over what was happening to him, and that bothered him.

At the police station, he stood at the charge bar and agreed to his name. He was told he would attend Ayr Sheriff Court the next day. The announcement seemed familiar. Until that time he would be regarded as innocent but remanded until he appeared at court.

Ronnie liked the word 'innocent' it fitted his reasoning.

'Come through this way,' said the desk sergeant, and Ronnie was led into a room where he was ordered to change into blue tracksuit bottoms and a blue T-shirt. 'Night wear,' said the policemen aware of his prisoner's mental condition. After all, the attire was for 'remand' prisoners as well as night sleepers. He looked at his watch. It was only 6 pm, too early to sleep.

A take-away meal of fish and chips arrived with a mug of cold milk.

'Thank you. This is very kind of you,' Ronnie said as his face lit up at the hot prepared evening meal. He ate the offering with a plastic spoon/fork. Not a breadcrumb was left.

An hour later, Ronnie felt very uncomfortable.

'Excuse me, is anyone there?'

Strange voices responded from nearby cells in a jocular manner. He called out again.

'Coming,' replied the night duty officer.

'Excuse me I'd like to go to the bathroom', he said politely, crossing his legs.

The policeman pointed to the corner of his cell. 'Over there. I'll bring some paper for you.'

Ronnie looked at where the officer pointed. It was not a familiar toilet. It seemed to have a lateral pipe leading outside the cell. There was no water in it. He looked at it confused.

'It filters drugs. Use it. I'll bring paper in a moment,' he said and turned to go. He walked away with his head turned back facing Ronnie's cell. He shouted for all to hear. 'No prisoner gets paper 'cause they dampen it with spit and throw it at the cell camera.'

Ronnie looked up to see a glass eye in the ceiling, focussing on him. He waved at it and produced a charming smile.

That night he could not get to sleep. The noise at times was deafening as drug users howled for their next fix in neighbouring cells and wails of anguish were heard from others waiting their fate the following morning. Ronnie found it hard to sleep on a stone bed with a sponge mattress and two blankets. He could not understand why he was there and the strangeness of the accommodation and atmosphere was completely beyond his experience.

He had to be disturbed at 7 am as the mug of tea and two slices of marmaladed toast arrived. He thanked his provider profusely, again. Breakfast in bed was not a feature of his life. It seemed a novelty.

A police van drove eight men to Ayr Sheriff court that morning. They chatted away in the back of the vehicle. Some bragged that this was a regular journey for them.

'What you up for, old man?' asked one.

Ronnie realised the question was addressed to him through his stare.

'I don't know,' he replied.

'Christ, you got no chance then,' he laughed.

'He's probably embarrassed to say anything. Probably a sex offender,' suggested another. Fortunately, Ronnie knew he was not a sex offender. He wondered why they thought he was one. He ignored the comment, still wondering why there were so many in the van.

The vehicle went to the back of the court where a strong wooden door opened to receive the alleged offenders. The occupants trotted out in line, after the strong door was closed of course, and waited. Ronnie still sat in the van. He was shouted to come out and realised he had upset the man offering him a hand to descend the van's steps.

He followed the men in line to a waiting room. At 9:55 am precisely they were led into the court and sat facing the bench. A few minutes later a side door opened and Sheriff Peter Hanks appeared.

'Court Rise,' shouted the former Army staff sergeant and the line of accused stood. Ronnie stood up moments later, hesitating like Lance Corporal Jones in Dad's Army. The sheriff took his seat and everyone sat down, except Ronnie. His sleeve was pulled down by the man sitting next to him and that placed him off balance for a moment before he returned to be properly seated.

One by one, the accused stood up when their name was called. Lean and tall with her hair tied back with a black and white hair band supporting her Ayr United football team, Procurator Fiscal Helen Lawrence introduced each case.

'Graham Anderson, a breach of the peace at the Ayr United v Morton game,' she said announcing the first case.

'How do you plead?' asked the sheriff.

'Guilty my lord, I got too excited at the match.'

'I am only interested in your guilty plea. I see you are a first-time offender. Well, that is in your favour. I am prepared to dismiss this case. Behave yourself in the future, at matches especially. I won't let you off so lightly next time. You are free to leave.'

'Thank you, Sheriff,' he said and left the court.

The fiscal slammed Anderson's file down on her desk. The Greenock Morton supporter had got off lightly in her mind. She lifted the next folder up and opened it.

'Gordon McLeod. Assault and bodily injury by pulling his wife's hair, shouting and swearing at her and throwing a lamp hitting her on the head causing her to have three stitches inserted at hospital.'

'Assault and Domestic abuse, yet another such case. How do you plead Mr. McLeod?

'Not guilty.'

The sheriff started to write. Then he looked up. The duty defence solicitor, Ranald Lawrie, was on his feet.

'My client is no longer living with his wife, My Lord. In these circumstances, I ask that he is not detained before his trial.'

The sheriff shook his head. 'I take a different view. He may not be living with his wife, but he may interfere with the evidence of his or her case, as is often seen in such offences. Gordon McLeod, you will be detained until your trial set for 7th June.'

The next folder was opened and the fiscal informed the sheriff of a speeding and drink driving charge.'

'And Mr. Anderson's speed element, Miss Lawrence?'

'34 mph in a 20 mile an hour zone at the Forehill Primary school, 24 Cessnock Place, Ayr.'

'How do you plead, Mr. Anderson?'

'I regret what I did.'

'So do I regret it, Mr. Anderson. But I asked you, how do you plead?' reiterated the sheriff.

'I am afraid so. Yes, I'm guilty.'

'One year probation. You will be supervised and undergo an alcohol awareness course and a speeding training course during this time. Any future drink driving offence will result in a custodial sentence. Do you understand? You are also banned from driving for nine months. Breach the conditions and you'll be back as quick as greased lightning to stand where you are at this very moment, for a different outcome. Am I making myself clear?'

'Yes, ma Lord.'

The accused moved along the wooden bench as their numbers dwindled.

'Mr. Ronald Jackson m' Lord charged with wasting police time' announced fiscal Helen Lawrence.

There was a moment when time stood still.

'Is he here?' asked the sheriff.

Ronnie received an elbow nudge. 'Hey, are you Ronald Jackson?' asked one of the accused.

Ronnie looked at him and nodded.

'Then stand up now.'

Ronnie took his advice and got to his feet. His eyes wandered around the court.

'Wasting police time. A serious offence,' remarked the sheriff.

'Yes, that is a serious offence,' Ronnie agreed.

The sheriff's eyes rose to assess his response. Was he being flippant?

'My lord, Mr. Jackson comes from Blackwaterfoot on Arran. The police report I have indicates he suffers from dementia,' Helen said, then sat down.

'Mr. Jackson. You are charged with wasting police time. How do you plead?'

'Yes, how do I plead? I don't know.'

The silence in the court was unusual.

Then Mr. Lawrie stood up. 'I am particularly interested in taking this case, my Lord.'

'Really?'

'Personal family reasons, your honour,' he revealed.

'I see, very well. Mental health is not a valid defence of course. You will need time to assess his responses I would think. It would also be convenient if he is detained at Kilmarnock prison till trial than to let him return to Arran where the offence took place.'

'I have no objection m'lord, 'said the confident and relieved landlubber solicitor, Mr. Lawrie.

'Very well, Mr. Jackson, Mr. Lawrie will be your solicitor. You will have to speak to him. So, I am detaining you at Kilmarnock prison in the meantime and until June 9th when your trial will take place. Do you understand?' the sheriff asked, in a clearly enunciated voice.

'I've not been to Kilmarnock for a long time. I can't remember where it is,' Ronnie said looking agitated.

4

Kilmarnock prison is a relatively new prison. It was airy and beds of summer flowers filled the borders in the escape-proof rectangle within its walls. Ronnie was placed in a cell with John Rawlins. John spoke with an educated accent and befriended Ronnie straight away. He too was in remand and naturally, a fellow inmate with dementia was preferred to a drug addict or violent prisoner he had feared would arrive that late afternoon to occupy and share his cell.

'So what offence are you facing?' John asked.

'They said wasting police time. I suppose Rory Murdoch did not believe me.'

'Who is Rory Murdoch?'

'He's the police sergeant at Lamlash. Do you not know him?'

'Arran? No, I don't know him. Then he will lead the evidence against you.'

Ronnie laughed. 'It's my word against his.'

'I'm facing a fraud charge.'

'Fraud? What's that?'

'Well, like you I am denying it. I hope to convince the jury I did not steal the money.'

'Are you a bank robber?'

John laughed. 'No, I ran a racket getting money from some elderly folk, and then I went on cruises. But some of my victims are quite old and I'm hoping by the time I get to trial, they may have died, or not want to testify. What do you think?'

'I don't know.'

'I guess you don't. How bad is your dementia?'

'Dementia? I am a postman on Arran.'

'You could have fooled me,' John said scratching his head. 'I was told you had dementia by the prison officer before you arrived.'

Ronnie looked at John and shook his head. 'People with dementia forget things, I don't forget.'

'I see,' said John realising dementia had many states of confusion.

Two days later solicitor Ranald Lawrie telephoned procurator fiscal Helen Lawrence at her office.

'Hi Helen, this case, you know Ronnie Jackson. He's a first-time alleged offender, a harmless soul with dementia. Are you not thinking of dropping the charge?'

'Come on Ranald. You know me better than that. I have to act in the interests of society. If I dropped the case and he continued to pester the police, my neck would be on the line.'

Ranald twisted the telephone cord around his index finger. 'Then what about going easy on summing up. You can persuade the jury it's a no-goer.'

'If only, Ranald. You go and interview him. See what his defence is and let's take it from there.'

'Okay, then no deal. I'll see him tomorrow,' he said dropping the phone onto its cradle. 'Damn,' he said to himself thumping his fist on the table. 'She didn't take the bloody bait.'

The following afternoon, Ronnie was getting the hang of a game of billiards. Three balls he could understand, not like the table of coloured balls on the snooker table also in the recreation centre of the prison.

As he lined his shot up for the centre pocket, his name was called out. He played the shot, and his eyes followed the ball into the pocket and out of sight.

'It's in,' he shouted.

'Mr. Jackson,' the voice shouted louder. 'A visitor.'

Ronnie was led into a small square room. It had no comforts just two chairs and a table. He noticed the table was secured to the floor by a chain and cement. Likewise, the chairs did not move. The door opened and Mr. Ranald Lawrie entered proffering his hand to shake Ronnie's.

'I am your solicitor, remember?'

'Yes, you were at the court, weren't you?' Ronnie responded then relaxed.

'Yes, that's right. Now, it's my job to get you out of here and back to Blackwaterfoot where you belong.'

Ronnie stood up. This was music to his ears, just what he wanted. 'Shall we go now?'

'Where?' asked the solicitor with a furrowed brow.

'Blackwaterfoot. Do you have a car?'

Ranald gestured for him to sit down again. 'It's not that simple, Ronnie. You sit down and let's see what we can do. First, do you know Mario Balan?'

'Balan, Balan, ah...yes Elena Balan is my home help and Mario does the garden. Yes, he comes to do the garden on some days.'

'What does he do at other times?

'He told me he works at the hotel.'

'What does he do there?'

'What does Mario do at the Kinloch hotel? I can't remember. But he put canes on my dahlias, I remember that.'

'You get on with him?'

'It's not easy, his English is not so good. I don't always understand him.'

Ranald wrote furiously on his padded notepaper.

'Why would he want to report you?'

'He wouldn't report me. I've done nothing to him,' said Ronnie with gathered eyebrows.

'Fact is he says you told him the drug dropping incidents were all in your mind, they did not exist.'

Ranald's statement met a blank face. Ronnie tried to make sense of what he had just heard. Part of it seemed true. He should explain that.

'Yes, of course, the incidents were in my mind. Where else would I store them? But they exist. They were real, I tell you, I saw it with my own eyes. Only Sergeant Murdoch does not believe me.'

'Trouble is Ronnie, there's no evidence of a boat being heard, the amounts of drugs have not been found and you keep telling Sergeant Murdoch of these occasions.'

'So, does that make me guilty?'

'Well Ronnie, it does not look good.' Ranald put his pen to his closed lips. He looked up at his client for a moment then tapped his pen on his pad. 'Ronnie, would you be willing to be my defence witness?'

'What does that mean?'

'After the procurator fiscal leads all her witnesses, I get a chance to lead my evidence, my witness. I have only got you. Are you up to some gentle questioning from me, or should we just try our luck and wing it with the jury?'

'If you want to make me speak, I'll tell the truth,' he said.

The interview lasted a further forty minutes interrupted by a tray of afternoon tea and biscuits.

When Ranald left Kilmarnock prison that afternoon, there was a spring in his step. Surely any jury would be influenced by a witness with dementia, unable to answer simple questions.

5

Refreshed and now very familiar with the court building, Ronnie returned to the seat at the table with his legal advisor. A whiff of garlic came from Ranald and Ronnie knew he was well fed for the fray about to follow. Then he was reminded he was the next witness.

The court was appropriately summonsed and the jury was in position. In the gallery were the local press. A male journalist from the Herald was present and the Scotsman was represented by a female journalist. Both opened their notepads prepared for an interesting article about to surface. Ronnie was told that there seemed to be much interest in his case. He smiled. That seemed good.

When all were present, Mr. Lawrie called Mr. Jackson to the witness box. Ronnie managed to take the oath but he held on to the Bible for his security.

Mr. Lawrie smiled at Ronnie before starting his questioning.

'Tell the court your name and age.'

'Yes, I am Ronald Jackson and I am aged er..er...I am 72. Yes, 72.'

'And where do you live?'

'I live at Blackwaterfoot. That's on Arran.'

'Yes, that's right. And I believe you are a retired postman. Not so?'

'Yes, I am a postman.'

'You were a postman Mr Jackson. You are not a postman now,' Ranald reminded him.

Ronnie felt reprimanded.

Oh, I see.'

'Tell me about the time you were the local postman. For example, when did you get up?'

'Yes, when I was a postman I had to get up very early.'

'And what time would that have been?' Ranald asked encouraging Ronnie with a nod.

'I had to be at the post office at 4 am so I got up at 3 15 in the morning.'

'And now you have retired, when do you get up?'

'At the same time.'

'You get up at 3:15 am and what do you do then?'

'I have a boiled egg and some toast, most days. A fried breakfast at the weekend.'

Ranald smiled as did Helen.

'And after breakfast where do you go?'

'I go for a walk.'

'Where?' asked Ranald getting a bit frustrated with Ronnie's pedantic responses.

'I go to the beach.'

'Now when you are at the beach at that very early time, have you ever seen anything unusual?'

Ronnie held on to the Bible and with his other hand, caressed its soft leather exterior. He recalled what he had seen.

'I sometimes see seals but not really many unusual things.'

'Not even a boat?'

Ronnie's eyes widened. He remembered why he was there. 'Oh yes, I've seen a boat come to the shore with drugs,' He said with enthusiasm.

'Take it slowly Mr. Jackson. Tell me about the boat, first.'

'It's dark red and white.'

'Okay I get the picture it's a dark red and white boat with an engine or a sail?'

'It has an engine but the engine is switched off when it reaches the shore.'

'What happens next?'

'One man stays on the boat and the other jumps off with two bags of drugs.'

'Now think carefully, how do you know the bags have drugs in them?'

Ronnie hesitated. Then he recalled. 'Because I've seen films about drugs arriving on islands. It's a good way to bring them. They do it often, I tell you.'

'How often have you seen this boat arrive and the man get out?'

'I think I told Sergeant Murdoch I've seen this three times. Maybe four. I don't know, I can't remember,' he replied scratching his head.

'Does the man return to the boat?'

'Yes, empty-handed. He has no bags then. And the engine starts and they go back out to sea.'

'So you have reported each time this happened, to Sergeant Murdoch?'

'Yes, but he does not believe me,' Ronnie said pulling his left sleeve down.

'And why is that?'

'Well, he did not bring dogs, or more police or the helicopter to see what I saw.'

Mr. Lawrie scribbled some notes on his papers.

'And if someone told you there was no boat and no drugs and no skipper and no runner, what would you say?'

'Umm...no boat? Then they would be telling a lie.'

'Now, about Mr. Mario Balan. You know him well?'

'His wife helps me about the house. She is my home help. She is a good help for me.'

'And Mario, her husband, how well do you know him?'

'I don't see so much of him. But he put canes in the ground to support my dahlias and chrysanthemums.'

'I see. And have you had conversations with him?'

'Yes, I speak to him sometimes.'

'Do you remember telling him, the boat and drugs were all lies?'

Ronnie looked around the court and then up to the gallery where the journalist's pens were poised to write.

'But that's not true; I saw the boat and bags of drugs. But if he says it's not true, then it's not true. Why would he lie?'

Ranald's heart missed a beat. He looked up at Ronnie and stared at him. 'Mr. Jackson, did you tell Mr. Balan there was neither boat nor drugs in existence?'

Ronnie clutched his fingers together. His solicitor was being serious.

'No, I did not tell him that. Because it's true. I saw the boat and men.'

'Thank you, Mr. Jackson, I have no further questions.'

Ronnie stepped down from the witness stand but Ranald told him to return for a moment.

'Miss Lawrence?' asked the sheriff.

Helen got to her feet.

'Just a couple of points of clarification, m'lord.'

'Very well,' he sighed placing his spectacles on his desk and ostentatiously looking at his wristwatch.

Ronnie lifted the Bible once more, expecting another oath.

'Please take the Bible away,' the sheriff requested the court official. 'Mr. Jackson, you are still under oath. You must continue to tell the truth. You understand?'

The court official approached the witness box and took the Bible from Ronnie's hands as he replied to the sheriff. 'Yes, I understand. I tell the truth.'

'Mr. Jackson, why did the sergeant not take you seriously? I mean, you were reporting a serious event,' asked Helen.

'I don't know.'

'You kept informing him, not so?'

'Yes, I told him many times about the boat.'

'Do you not think by constantly bothering the sergeant, he might charge you with wasting police time?'

'No, I wanted him to investigate.'

'Let me return to Mr. Balan. Do you like him?'

'Umm...I don't know. I don't always understand him.'

The sheriff drummed his pen on his ink pad sufficient to attract Helen's attention to inform her he was becoming further exasperated.

'Well, you employ him to work in your garden. Is that not a good arrangement?'

'Yes, that's a good arrangement.'

'You have had no arguments with him?'

'No, no arguments with him,' Ronnie repeated.

'So he had no axe to grind as it were?'

Ronnie's mind was elsewhere, seemingly gazing up at the journalists once more.

'I put it to you that Mr. Balan was only doing his duty so that the police would know you were telling lies.'

'I don't tell lies,' Ronnie said shaking his head from side to side.

'I have no further questions,' said Helen, taking her seat, having completed her re-examination.

The learned sheriff scribbled some notes before addressing the jury.

'Members of the jury, you have heard the evidence of this case. We will now have a summing up, first by the Procurator Fiscal and then by Mr. Jackson's solicitor. Miss Lawrence, are you prepared?'

'Indeed milord,' Helen said as she gathered her papers in order. 'Ladies and gentlemen of the jury, the law of the land is fair. The mental health of the accused is not for you to consider or question even although there have been several occasions where you will have identified Mr. Jackson's illness. I ask you to concentrate on the police officer's actions. He took account of Mr. Jackson's information, and, recognising his condition, even contacted social services in order to assist Mr. Jackson in living with dementia. But when independent evidence emerged from Mr. Balan, the case took on a more formal outlook. Could we possibly expect a fifth or sixth time of reporting by Mr. Jackson? Was there not a limit to the officer's time spent recording Mr. Jackson's allegations? And surely the sergeant would have known if there was a drugs cartel operating in rural Arran at Blackwaterfoot, in particular? As a fiscal, I have certainly never had a major drug case from peaceful Arran. So, something had to be done to stop this from becoming a fixation, a conditioned response, a drain on police time. I need not tell you the gravity of the charge of Wasting Police Time.

You may do so with a heavy heart, but the right thing must be done. I invite you to return a verdict of guilty. Thank you,' she concluded and promptly sat down.

Mr. Lawrie stood up. 'Ladies and gentlemen of the jury, by the grace of God go you and me. We cannot see the future but almost certainly there are at least 7 in 100 sufferers aged 65, and, in 39 cases in 100 for those over the age of 80 who will suffer dementia and its other forms. Accordingly, some of you in this courthouse will suffer dementia or Alzheimer's disease before too long or have relatives with this dastardly disease. For that's what it is. That is a fact. My friend rightly informed you that mental health is not an excuse to turn a blind eye.

The case must be heard and it has been. But I put it to you, that Sergeant Murdoch could have done more. The problem was that he lives in Lamlash as do his officers, well some in Brodick, and they don't have postman's hours. Such hours understandably are the twilight hours when crime is most active, yet, no undercover operation took place. Had it done so, then perhaps a major drug-running incident would have begun but it didn't.

The opportunity was not taken; was lost perhaps and that made Mr. Jackson a pain in the, well, neck I suppose. Mr. Balan, a semi-literate English speaker. Why would he report Mr. Jackson? That has not been made clear. There had been no rift. They got on amicably as best they could. I put it to you that Mr. Balan mistook whatever Mr. Jackson said and he reported what was on his mind and not what he heard from Mr. Jackson's lips.

You are asked to consider my client's guilt on the basis of being beyond reasonable doubt. This case is full of doubts, reasonable doubts. Doubt why Mr. Jackson was not believed, doubt surrounding Sergeant Murdoch's investigation, doubt whether Mr. Balan heard correctly, and doubt that my client, such an ill man with dementia, and a first-time alleged offender I remind you, was properly regarded by the police as a very ill man. With these mounting doubts, I urge you to find my client, Mr. Jackson, not guilty. I thank you for your patience and pray that none of you become afflicted in such a way as my client.'

Ranald sat down and patted Ronnie's arm gently.

A hush came over the proceedings as the jurors prepared their arguments, the Fiscal gathered her papers, Ranald put his pen in his jacket pocket and the accused smiled generously at the whole court.

'Ladies and gentlemen of the jury,' began Sheriff Constance. 'I must ask you to retire to make your decision. You must do so as Mr. Jackson stated; to find the evidence of the charge on the balance of probability, if it exists, and you must also remember, above all, mental health cannot be a mitigating factor in your decision.'

6

Eighty minutes later word circulated that the jury had made their decision. The press jostled to find the best vantage point. Helen returned to her place at the table as did Ranald and Ronnie sauntered in, a man without any obvious concern, and greeted Ranald with a thumping handshake, like a long-lost friend.

'Take it easy Ronnie. Be prepared for the worst and the best sometimes happens.' Then he smiled at his client. 'Mark my word. I feel we have won.'

'Yes, we have won,' repeated Ronnie.

Sheriff Constance took his place on the bench and proceedings were called to order.

'Madam Juror, have you reached a decision ?'

'We have m'lord,' she said rather nervously.

The sheriff asked the Jury chairman to read the verdict.

'By majority, we find the defendant guilty.'

There was a gasp of astonishment around the court from many in the public gallery. Sheriff Constance silenced the outburst with a sharp look around his court with pouted lips and a frown.

'And that is the verdict of the jury?'

Heads nodded.

'Please stand Mr. Jackson.'

Ronnie did as he was asked and Ranald held his breath.

'The jury has reached a majority decision, one that I am satisfied to deliver. Mr. Jackson you have been found guilty of wasting police time. I sentence you, Mr. Jackson, to six months imprisonment, with the time spent on remand being deducted from the sentence. That is all. Thank you.'

'Thank you,' said Ronnie respectfully as his prison officer approached bearing handcuffs.

Ranald raised his hand. 'These are hardly necessary. You won't find a more polite man than my client.'

'Rules, Mr. Lawrie, just rules.'

Ronnie returned to Kilmarnock prison but not on the remand wing. He was led into a changing room where an orange sweatshirt was supplied with grey joggers. He was then taken to the mature wing where offenders over the age of sixty were detained. He learned that for their security, the elderly sex offenders were held on another wing and so his cellmate was a 67-year-old man serving three years for burglary.

Drew Pender was unsure how a prisoner, his new cellmate with dementia would be. He would soon know. But it would take some time for them to get along and understand each other.

Arran is primarily a holiday island. It always has been and always will be. That was why a Lancashire couple felt an island break would fit the bill for them. They chose a self-catering home in Blackwaterfoot looking across the bay. Eric Williams was the owner of a garage and his wife, Gail, was a retail assistant in a dress shop in Wigan. They had a son, Peter. He left school two years ago and drifted from one job to another. This was a source of annoyance as Eric was approaching retirement with an ongoing business sitting on a plate if his son would only accept the work.

Their holiday got off to a good start. Eric and Sandra un-woundon the beach, walked to the King's cave, they played golf at the Shiskine Golf course, they visited the Holy Isle and they restocked at the Co-op in Brodick on the way home. But at night, a niggle festered.

Ronnie was not depressed. He saw his new accommodation as acceptable and had a new friend. The food was perhaps not plentiful but he found it tasty and regular and it was prepared for him.

At the Herald office, they were set to run the trial and its conclusion but the journalist, Stan Bell was ill at ease. He could not see how a jury could find Ronnie guilty, especially by a majority. Yet he had to report the case as it was recorded. He went to his feature editor.

'That Arran guy with dementia. Even if he was guilty, prison is not the place he should be.' He began strolling to a seat in the editor's room.

Editor Paul Duncan listened. He always had time for Stan.

'Dementia and prison don't fit well together,' said Stan getting into his stride.

'So?'

'I've been thinking. If we could do an article about mental health in Scottish prisons, we could put it in a weekend supplement. What do you think?'

Paul nodded. 'I like that idea. Are you busy at present?'

'I could start it next week if you like,' said Stan feeling he was seeing a clear green light ahead.

'Okay, see what you come up with,' he said to Stan's delight.

Ronnie sat on his bed swinging his legs. He looked over to Drew. 'I'm a postman. I get up early to go to the office and collect the mail,' he said.

Drew looked at his cellmate in surprise. 'What! You still working? I mean you ain't sacked?' he said his voice rising on both sentences.

His question was met with silence.'

'What are you here for anyway? Theft of mailbags?' Drew suggested.

'No. I'm here because the sheriff sent me here.'

'Yea, I know that. But what did you do, to get here?' he asked impatiently.

'I don't really know. I mean they say I told a lie but I didn't. I saw them bring drugs to the shore. Trouble was Sergeant Murdoch didn't believe me, so he charged me with wasting his time.'

'So wasting police time. I see,' he said shaking his head in disbelief.

'And why are you here?' asked Ronnie.

'I've been a burglar for years. Never caught me till last year. I'm getting lazy. I'm leaving evidence wherever I go these days. I reckon this will be my last sentence. I'll not do it again.'

'Neither will I unless I see the boat again.'

Eric and Gail Williams had a meal at the Kinloch hotel. Their conversation centred on their lazy son, Peter. He was the stepson of Eric and son of Gail, from an earlier marriage. Peter was now approaching his twentieth birthday and without a regular job.

'Ye know luv, he can never stick with a job. Always onto sumthing new, like. How can he gain any experience? Eh? I will retire soon. So, do I sell garage? No, I want him to take it over. Keep it going, serving Lancastrians, like my father and his father did all those years ago, like. It's a family business, a family tradition, you know that luv,' he said in his Wigan twang.

'He'll find sumthing and settle down. I'm sure of that,' said Gail.

'No, he won't. He can't settle down. He's never been a hard worker. He thinks life owes him sumthing,' snarled Eric.

'Eee, that's harsh. He's tried a few jobs and been paid well like,' she responded in her son's defence.

'What he needs is slap in face with wet fish, does he.'

Eric finished his glass of beer. He raised his hand and ordered an Arran whisky. It was to be the first of three and before his final glass was empty, Gail had long since returned to their holiday home.

The bar was closing and the bartender asked him to retire as the hotel was being closed down for the night. Eric stood up, went to the loo then hit the fresh cool air of the dark sky-sparkling Arran night.

As he walked back to the self-catering cottage, he looked out to sea. The fresh wind blew his hair backwards and seemed to revive him from his drunken stupor. He saw a light on the water. It began to move towards the shore. He stood watching it. Funny time to be out he thought. He had been seen. He waved to the boat. There was no response except the boat turned around and went back out into the Kilbrannan Sound.

7

Stan Bell rang the Scottish Prison Service to gain some facts about prisoners with dementia. The Freedom of Information prison sites were made readily available on-line and he devoured them. His article took shape and he knew what he had to write would create interest.

At Kilmarnock prison, Drew and Ronnie sat at their breakfast table. Pale scrambled eggs on toast were what Ronnie ate. Drew held a plastic mug of hot tea in both hands. 'So you got six months, that right.'

'Six months but with a few days less, because...er....because the sheriff told me.'

'Those would be your pre-trial remand days.'

'I see.'

'But you won't do six months,' Drew said with a heavy heart.

Ronnie looked terrified. 'I can't escape. I don't want to.'

Drew laughed so loudly he was ordered to keep the noise down.

'Ronnie, you have excellent behaviour; that will shorten your sentence. You can look to be out in two months. That's nothing. You'll be home soon.'

'Home at Blackwaterfoot?'

'Yea, that's where you are from, isn't it?'

'But I'm in Kilmarnock now, not so?'

Drew smiled inanely. 'Yes we live in Kilmarnock,' he laughed and Ronnie laughed too. Though he was not sure why.

Eric Williams received a rollicking from his wife Gail for drinking to excess, the next morning. He was apologetic blaming his stepson's attitude as the source of his drinking weakness. When the tension in the relationship subsided, he changed the subject. 'I saw boat last night, I know, you think I was drunk, but I did see it like. It did a strange thing. It seemed to see me watching it. I waved to it, you know. Then suddenly it turned around and went away.'

'Well it would at that time of night, wouldn't it? Heading back home sumwhere after a night of fishing I presume.'

Eric stroked his chin with his fingers feeling his growth required a shave. 'Ah suppose so, luv,' was all he said.

The following weekend, Stan Bell had his article Dementia in Cells published in the paper's weekend supplement. His writing generated many responses in the following day's letters pages as Stan questioned the appropriateness of a first-time dementia offender currently in Kilmarnock prison for wasting police time. Some went as far as to question if the presiding sheriff, Sheriff Constance, had not overstepped the mark in his sentencing. But no appeal was forthcoming from Ranald Lawrie's office. Following this report, the Arran Banner editor Hugh Boag took up the case in the local paper and drummed up support for the former postman.

As usual, Erik got up to go to the loo at 4 am and on his way back to bed, he looked out of the window. He rubbed his eyes. Then he focussed on what seemed to be the same boat he had seen a few nights ago, make its way to the Blackwaterfoot slipway. A man got out with two bags and ran towards town. He lost sight of him but he saw the boat skilfully turn round and await his seagoing passenger. He would have thought nothing of it. Perhaps an early delivered vegetable or bread drop but the man running back to the boat, not only looked back several times, he seemed to have a neck warmer pulled over his mouth as well as a dark skip cap. He must have felt unnoticed, but Eric got his description, down to his white socks.

Eric was anxious to wake his wife and inform her of what he had seen but he really did not want to see her anger for a second time this holiday, so he retreated to bed and was soon fast asleep.

The next morning at breakfast Eric told his wife what he saw and her response was to mind his own business. This was an island affair. Not a Lancashire matter to get involved with.

'You want to return to court here in Scotland to give evidence and lose muney from the garage, luv?'

Erik nodded. Staying silent seemed the thing to do.

Over morning toast, Rory opened his weekend Herald and his eyes set on Dementia in Cells, the article written by Stan Bell. As he read more, his thoughts turned to Ronnie who by then had served a month in Kilmarnock prison. Out soon before too long, he thought. Better not upset the apple cart. Yet Rory was ill at ease. He had gone on Mario's firm evidence to convict the postman but had he bent over enough to help Ronnie? What if there was some truth in what he told him? He drank some more of his Guatemalan coffee which he held cupped in his two hands. Then he sat back for a few mouthful moments, closed the paper and went to his telephone.

'Hi Pete, missing the force?'

'Hi Rory, at times. Mind you not the shift work,' he laughed raucously.

'Doing anything else these days?' Rory asked in a floating question.

'At Blackwaterfoot? No, just daily golf, read the paper, walk the dog. I'm 60 past you know. I did 41 years in uniform. Much more comfortable in my Pringle jerseys around the course these days,' he laughed as he remembered some good pitched shots around the greens.

Rory laughed too, imagining the golfing days he'd enjoy before too long. 'Thing is, I have a hunch.'

'Oh dear not getting me back to the force, I hope.'

'No, no not that. It's your location. Your bungalow looking over the slipway.'

'What are you talking about?' Pete asked scratching the back of his head.

'I want to put my mind at ease. See if there's any foul play on this patch. Maybe it's nothing. What I'd like is for me to be in your attic for a couple of nights. How do you feel about that?'

'I suppose you can. Angie won't mind if it's you in the attic,' he laughed. 'Dog's getting deaf. He won't be a problem. So you want a bed in the attic?'

'Don't go to any lengths. Even just somewhere by the window where I can see the slipway.'

'When are you thinking?'

'Well Pete, providing Angie agrees. I'd like two nights. Next Tuesday and Thursday should be good days.'

'Okay, why don't you come round for a meal at 7 30 pm on Tuesday and then get set up?' said Pete feeling it a long time since they had a guest to dine.

'That's very kind of you, indeed. I guess if anything happens it will be nearer 4 am.'

'You need an alarm call too?'

Ronnie and Drew were regular billiard players and the days seemed to pass remarkably well at the posh Kilmarnock prison estate. Many prisoners took the Mickey out of Ronnie but his dementia always gave his adversaries a forgiving smile. Drew understood Ronnie best and when Ronnie relapsed, he was supportive.

'Why am I here,' asked Ronnie.

'We are having a wee break Ronnie. All of us are. So enjoy it.'

'I do,' he replied repositioning the cue ball.

9

After eating a sumptuous meal, Angie announced that she had set up a table with a kettle for tea or coffee and a tin of biscuits if Rory got hungry. 'And there's a loo on the landing below. You won't disturb us I assure you,' Angie said. 'We are both sound sleepers,' she laughed. 'Let's hope it's a profitable outcome.'

'If it is, it will hit the press big time. I'm sure of that,' said Rory.

Rory sat down and made himself comfortable in the attic. In the moonlight, he was able to re-read the article by Stan Bell. He read that some 8% of prisoners suffered from Dementia. But in the over 60 age group, it rose to 27% with varying degrees of forgetfulness ranging from incidents from mild cognitive impairment to dementia and Alzheimer's cases. The more he read, the more he felt that some offending must be mental health related. It was a matter which the courts should take into account more fully, he thought, especially with the more minor of offences.

He pulled up his left sleeve and looked at his wristwatch. It was approaching 1 a.m. He looked outside. The atmosphere was calm and still. Not a sound of human activity was about. Only the hoot of an owl disturbed the peace every so often at Blackwaterfoot that night, at that eerie late hour.

By 3.30 am Rory was wide awake. Adrenalin coursed through his veins as his eyes peered through his binoculars into the inky sea. But there was no activity. There was still no-one of interest by 5 am when his eyelids closed and he fell asleep.

Two days later he returned to undertake his silent observation but again no boat arrived and he once more thought Ronnie's sightings came from the recesses of a damaged brain and not reality. He informed his hosts, Peter and Angie that he would make no more nocturnal observations from their home.

Three days later, Peter had a late night with friends at the Kinloch hotel and could not get to sleep. He eventually did but as it approached 4 am, his regular visit to the loo took place. After washing his hands with a cake of white Dove soap and drying them on a warm deep-piled pink towel, he decided to return to where Rory had been on observation.

He polished his glasses on his pyjama jacket then sat on the chair in the roof-top attic. He focussed his eyes on the slipway harbour. Three boats were already tied up, but a fourth craft was entering the secure basin with a man in white socks about to step off. He did so clutching one bag.

Peter now had two aspects to watch. First, the boat as it silently turned round ready to depart and the man heading up the slight hill. He was seen to take a right turn beyond the hotel and moments later he returned empty-handed. Peter's police instinct took effect. He was not sure how big this could turn out to be but his sixth sense told him, he had to proceed with caution, gain facts before approaching his former colleague, or possibly be rebuffed for getting too involved. Nevertheless, Peter took a note of the men's description as well as the boat. It was 4:05 am.

At 8:30 later that morning, Pete went to the Kinloch hotel and asked for the manager, Mr. Robbie Crawford.

'Hi, can I have a moment of your time?'

'Sure Pete, something on your mind? Let's sit over here,' he said with a sweeping gesture of his hand. 'Mary, two coffees, please. Err.... coffee for you is in order?' he asked Pete.

'Yes, coffee at this time of the day's just fine, flat white if I can?'

'Got that Mary?'

'Yes, sir,' she replied and twirled around and disappeared towards the kitchen.

'Well, tell me what's on your mind?' asked Robbie.

'A sensitive one. I have been acting undercover.......'

'Hang on. I thought you retired from the Polis?'

'Yes I did but you know, once a policeman always one. Anyway, I observed a drug drop. Almost sure it is. A boat dropped off a man and he returned moments later from the rear of the hotel. Either he left the bag there for someone to pick it up later, or he handed it to someone at the back of the hotel. You following me?'

'So far,' said Robbie adjusting his forward-leaning position in his chair. 'You mean it could be a staff member involved?'

'Possibly. Do you have a night watchman?'

'Well, we have an odd-job man, a useful sort of guy. He's a sort of night watchman. No need for a night watchman here, usually.'

'Before I know more about him, do you mind me checking the back of the hotel with you, just in case the drugs are still there?'

'No problem, let's go.'

As they stood up, Mary arrived with a tray of coffees and buttered scones.

'Just leave them there thanks, we'll be back shortly,' said an apologetic Robbie.

The two men arrived at the back of the building through the kitchen. Pete overturned two plastic empty tubs, but there was nothing there, of interest. He circumvented the area methodically. With his hand, he peered into a couple of bushes, but they produced nothing. It took the best part of fifteen minutes, although nothing was found, to satisfy himself that someone must have been there to collect the bag of drugs.

`I think that coffee must be waiting for us now,' Pete said.

Robbie nodded but his mind was elsewhere. `The night watchman/odd-job guy, you want to know about. He is called Mario Balan, he's Romanian,' the manager said.

'Okay, say nothing about this to anyone,' said Pete recalling one of his police lines committed to memory. 'And didn't I see a scone with the coffee?'

Pete returned to his home and took a sheet of paper to record what he had observed and learned. He telephoned Rory. He was out but an urgent message was relayed to Rory's mobile phone. Rory phoned back almost immediately.

'Hi Rory, you busy?'

'Not really. Cars smashed at Lochranza. Ambulance just arrived.'

'Well, I've some intelligence for you. There is a drug smuggling issue in Blackwaterfoot.'

'What! You are kidding me.'

'No, I had a 4 am vigil like you and saw the boat enter the slipway. This guy got out with a bag and went behind the hotel where he left the drugs probably with a staff member. The guy was dressed in black with white socks.'

'You saw all this?'

'Enough to warrant an enquiry, I thought. So I went to see the manager, you know Robbie Crawford, a delightful fellow. He told me the name of a man who could help with your enquiries. Or you may want to catch him red-handed yourself. That's up to you.'

Rory turned his back on the car accident.

'Pete can you give me a written statement about all you saw?' asked Rory clenching his fist in excitement.

'No problem.'

'Oh, and you said you had a name?' Rory asked holding his breath.

'Yes, I had to write that down. Foreign he is. He's from Romania, you probably don't know him. He's Mario Balan.'

'Know him? His evidence got Ronnie behind bars. Now I see why he wanted to get Ronnie out of the way. Okay, I've some telephone calls to make, urgently. Pete, I wish you never retired from the force.'

'You must be kidding.' I'd be missing years of golfing if I did.'

10

Ronnie was told by staff he had only two weeks left of his sentence. Ronnie never referred to being in prison as a sentence and was unsure why he was being told this.

`I like it here. I like the billiards, the friends I have, so I'm not going anywhere.'

The staff made an appointment for Ronnie to adjust back home at Blackwaterfoot the following day and at the end of the session, he was beginning to see Kilmarnock prison no longer wanted him. He recalled his home and wondered why he had not gone back sooner. The staff had listened to him but did not engage in answering his lines of communication when they were so surreal and vague.

Rory contacted the Ayrshire mainland Police Scotland to discuss the developing case with Superintendent Roy Fraser.

'Okay, we have a lot to do. First, I'll apply the 5x5x5.'

'5x5x5 sir?'

'The model grades. The source of the intelligence. You should remember. It evaluates the information you have provided as a score of 1 to 5 and on the same basis indicates who has access to the information. PROTECT,

RESTRICTED, CONFIDENTIAL, SECRET and TOP SECRET.'

'Sorry sir, I wasn't thinking. Of course, it's all coming back to me. I guess it's because I'm an Arran cop,' he said feeling sheepish.

'I'll contact S.I.D *(Scottish Intelligence Database)* and Marine Scotland Police who can track all boats in the area. You, Rory, contact the Fishing Mission for port news but first, we must get authority for surveillance from R.I.P.S.A *(Regulation of Investigatory Powers Scotland Act (Scotland) 2000.)*'

'Okay, I see. So how long will that take?'

'When are you planning the strike?'

'Next week? Mid-week?'

'Authority should be given before then but I have to ensure it's a cost-effective mission. You say about a 4 am strike?'

'Yes, that's the time they seem to drop the drugs off.'

'We could bring forward the early shift by a couple of hours and the late shift can do two hours overtime. I could justify that expense.'

'Good. I'll keep costs down at my end if I can.'

'By the way, how regular are the drops?'

'Err... they seem to be either on Tuesdays and Thursdays for a two-week drop or Wednesday if it's a one-day drop.'

'Okay, we go for next Tuesday. I'll deploy plain-clothes detectives at Pete's house, and two officers in

Number 2s behind the hotel. Can they be hidden there?' asked Roy Fraser.

'Yes, there's enough garbage and bushes. I'll send a photo to you of the rear of the hotel.'

'Good. I'll authorise the use of tasers for four officers. Make sure the press are away from the location, at this stage.'

'Yup,'

'Oh and that Ronnie guy in Kilmarnock prison, get that sorted out pronto,' said Fraser. 'We don't want egg on our faces.'

'Certainly, that's a priority,' said Rory thumping his fist on his knee.

'Tomorrow, can you come over for a planning brief? Can you make it for 10 am?'

'Early sailing. No problem.'

Rory put down the phone for only a second. He lifted it again and dialled Helen Lawrence, the procurator fiscal.

'Developments Helen, developments. The bottom line is Ronnie Jackson, you know the Kilmarnock prisoner?....'

'Of course, how could I forget that case? He must be due out quite soon.'

'Well, he's innocent. We are about to charge the drug couriers, pick-up the others and God knows what else will follow. One thing for certain is that Ronnie Jackson was telling the truth all along.'

'Wow, Christ no-one expected that. Right, I'll get Ronnie to court tomorrow to quash his conviction. Let me get on to that right away.'

'Great. But I don't want Ronnie around for the next week. He could destroy what we have planned. He's an early riser and bound to interfere with our early morning lying in wait.'

'Okay, we'll break our budget but who cares? He deserves a break too.'

Ronnie was approached by the Kilmarnock Governor when he was resting in his cell.

Ronnie got up to welcome him, as he did to all officers visiting his caged abode. 'Be seated, Ronnie. Drew, can you leave us a moment?' asked the governor.

'I want him to stay. He's my friend,' Ronnie said urgently and plead with eyes of worry.

'Very well Drew, but you must not interrupt what I have to say to Ronnie.'

'No sir,' replied Drew.

'There's been a development in your case Ronnie. The police are now convinced you were telling the truth at your trial.'

'I always tell the truth.'

'Yes, that is plain to see. Ronnie, you will be taken to court again tomorrow where your sentence will be revoked, I mean quashed. It means you will be a free man.'

'Can I speak?' asked Drew.

The Governor nodded his agreement.

'Well done Ronnie. I'll miss you.'

'But I'll still play billiards with you,' said Ronnie with crestfallen spirits.

'Not here you won't. You are going home, you lucky thing,' Drew said patting his back.

The governor shook his head.

'Well, not quite. After court, you will be taken to the Fairfield House Hotel for a week. A re-integration into civilian life.'

'Hey, sir, so that's how you leave the prison these days. I can't wait for that treatment. But I'll put money on that you won't give me that treatment when I leave, will you?' said a smiling Drew with a wicked eye.

'No I'm afraid not. We are giving you this treatment, Ronnie, all free of charge, because you deserve it for one thing, but also because there is a police operation taking place soon at Blackwaterfoot and it's best you are not around.'

'Oh, I see. Will they send a helicopter?'

'I don't know how they will do it Ronnie, but I am sure they would have thought about that.'

'They will need a helicopter surely won't they, Drew?'

'Suppose they will,' Drew said to keep Ronnie content.

'Now, about the hotel two things I must mention. An NHS staff nurse will be with you during the day and there is a swimming pool for your enjoyment too.'

'Swimming pool,' said Ronnie closing his eyes in distress and grimacing as he took a breath. 'I've not brought my swimming trunks.'

Drew laughed. The governor smiled. 'They'll sort that out too, I'm sure.'

The following morning the Governor drove Ronnie to court after a fond farewell to Drew.

Ronnie knew exactly where he was once more but Helen led him not into the court.

'We're going to go to the sheriff's chambers. This won't take long.'

Sheriff Peter Hanks was already seated at his oak table in a well-upholstered leather chair. Helen asked Ronnie to be seated and she remained seated too. The formality of the usual legal proceedings seemed to have vanished. Ronnie wondered why no court official was shouting for the court to rise. Instead, the sheriff addressed Ronnie directly.

'Mr Jackson.' Ronnie stood up immediately having heard his name called.

'Please remain seated. This is not a trial. Indeed I am pleased to meet you again. In fact, it should be a very happy day for you, Mr. Jackson. Not so?'

'I'm not allowed to play billiards any more,' he responded with bloodhound eyes.

'I see. No billiards. Tell me about Kilmarnock prison. How did you cope?' asked the sheriff as Helen sat happily beside her client.

'It was good. I made a few friends.'

'I'm pleased to hear it. But you will be going home to your friends at Blackwaterfoot very soon now.'

Helen raised her hand. 'My Lord, there is an ongoing police investigation at Blackwaterfoot starting early next week. It is felt Mr. Jackson should not be in the vicinity during this event, for his safety, of course. We have made arrangements for Mr Jackson. He will be at the Fairfield House Hotel, in Ayr with a nurse to attend to his needs,' stated Helen with a sympathetic smile at Ronnie.

'The Fairfield? Well well, well, that's where I play bridge. It is a beautiful hotel. There's even a swimming pool there. You will enjoy your time at the hotel,' said the relaxed smiling sheriff.

'Yes, I am sure I will enjoy my time there,' said Ronnie. 'But I have no swimming costume.'

The sheriff put his hand into his suit pocket, brought out his black leather wallet and produced two twenty pound notes. 'Here, this should get you the finest pair of swimming trunks in town,' he suggested with a wide-eyed smile.

Helen saw the money. 'It will certainly provide a stunning pair of trunks, m'lord.'

'Now Mr Jackson, there is just one other matter. You have served time in prison as an innocent man. I am sure Madam fiscal you will expedite a claim to the Criminal Justices Board to consider the appropriate financial recompense for his false imprisonment?'

'Indeed my Lord that will be initiated this afternoon.'

'It means a large sum of money is coming your way, Mr. Jackson. Use it wisely but use it for your pleasure too, is my advice.'

'We will make arrangements for the money to be properly allocated to his bank account,' said Helen tapping Ronnie's arm gently.

'I am obliged. Well, that is the business over. You are free to leave this court at Ayr for the very last time,' said Sheriff Hanks who stood up and walked around the table to shake Ronnie's hand.

10

Fairfield House Hotel was welcoming and Gwen his nurse was quick to identify herself. She would have a room next door to Ronnie's and they got on like the proverbial house on fire. Ronnie enjoyed some sumptuous meals in her company and every day he appeared by the poolside in Mediterranean patterned swimming briefs, just as the sheriff had anticipated.

Mid-week Gwen drove Ronnie to the South Sands at Troon and then to the Piersland Hotel for afternoon tea. All was well with the world on Ronnie's mainland while at his home in Blackwaterfoot; there was an eerie calmness about the shore.

All permission sought by legislation and over-time arrangements had been approved. The Fishing Mission report gave a count-down of all registered boats in neighbouring harbours. That would provide additional and excellent evidence as would the boatman's mobile when seized. It would have the ports where the boat had been, stored in its location setting.

Two officers were comfortably ensconced behind the hotel an hour after midnight. Two plain-clothed officers were in the hotel, near the bay window with an eye to the sea. Hotel manager Robbie Crawford ensured his residents were out of the way and the police officers received all creature comforts. The coffee percolated happily on the sideboard under four anthropomorphic paintings. And at the bar, a platter of seafood and sandwiches were available during breaks.

Robbie ensured his staff, except Mario who had earned a few days' leave he had been told, was aware of the police presence and the need for total secrecy. He had great confidence in them that night, as always.

Meanwhile, two other officers were in Pete and Angie's attic where they relaxed with cups of tea and biscuits well into the morning hours. Their comfort was not enjoyed by a lone warm-suited aqua diver hidden in his black camouflaged attire in the unfortunate shortest grass on the bank of the slipway. Yet the darkness and his attire made him invisible. All were in communication for the time being.

At the crossroads, almost a mile from the town, a police van hidden by a field's hedge, awaited its part in the arrests. Cows in the field showed a casual interest in the human movement in the van. Time ticked on and on.

At 5:30 am on that Wednesday morning, Ronnie put out a message to everyone in position. 'Abort mission. Re-assemble midnight.....Thursday night.'

He could hear the disappointment in their responses but for some, another day of overtime was good recompense.

Rory had told the assembled officers that the preparation for a second ambush would be maintained as was for the first, but it would be the last time the force could undergo this costly exercise.

The night's operation had been approved for the Thursday night and so they returned then, and the officers took up their positions once more. Rory found himself praying it would be a success. If the drug runners changed their day, then he could not guarantee they would be caught this way. A lot was resting on arrests this night.

At 3:40 am a gentle purr could be heard. It came from out of a choppy sea. Rory strained his eyes to confirm what he hoped, then gave his penultimate command. 'To all. Boat seen approaching. Be alert and good luck. Any questions? Be quick?'

Rory waited a full two minutes. 'Okay, all in order. Let's make it a clean capture. Good luck guys. Switch off all mobiles.'

Rory looked through his binoculars. He saw two men now. They were neither particularly tall nor powerful, which was a good omen.

The boat's engine died as the craft drifted into the harbour. One man, wearing white socks, stood ready to jump. As soon as he was on dry land and making for the hotel, the officer in his camouflaged dark aqua suit slid down the shallow bank and shouted, 'Freeze, Police !'

On hearing this, the engine revved and the boat spun round. The officer shouted to the skipper. 'Stop or be tasered.' The boat was now in position to leave the mouth of the harbour. The officer was already wading through the shallow water. 'Stop or I fire,' was heard from where Rory was and his heart was in his mouth. Had an arrest been frustrated?

The officer fired his taser and the skipper collapsed like a sack of potatoes onto the deck. The officer got to the boat and climbed aboard as the boat began to circle round and round. Making his handcuffs secure on the man, and becoming dizzy as he did so, he managed to switch off the engine and brought his man to the shore. Another officer took over from him, forcing the skipper face-down on the grassy bank while voices were heard from the back of the hotel. Rory having seen the harbour arrest ordered the police van to approach and collect the detained skipper.

At the back of the hotel, two policemen had made their presence known and two men were now lying face down with a bag between both bodies. They telephoned Rory to say that two men and a bag of presumed drugs had been seized. 'Both men are subdued and ready for collection, sir.'

Rory assessed the situation. Both men seized. But he had to gather more evidence. He could do that without the men. He told them to proceed with caution on a job well done.

Rory made his way to the captured skipper.

'Where's, your phone?'

The man pretended not to understand.

'Well fortunately it's too early and no-one is around. Officer strip-search the man naked and find his phone.'

'It's in my pocket,' he said fearing a strip search and revealing he had command of the English language. Little did he know that an intimate search would come later.

With all the accused in transport and the other officers preparing to leave, Rory went down to the slipway. As he inspected the boat before boarding it, he noticed the name on the side of the boat. "Glad Tidings". He grinned at the inappropriate name. On closer inspection underneath the name was a previous name. He went closer to read it. Sk-la-k II had been scrapped and substituted but the old name was still partially visible. Using his crossword skills Rory decided this was the Skylark II. He'd soon find out where it came from.

He phoned the Marine Scotland Police.

'A check on the Skylark II, please.'

'This will take a moment, sir.'

'I'll wait,' said Rory and he did for at least three minutes.

'Skylark I and Skylark III are both registered in Oban, but interestingly Skylark II was reported stolen five months ago. Is it sailing under a new name?'

'I'm not surprised with that information but it will open up this case. Then I reckon the boat we have here is the Skylark II going under the name of Glad Tidings. Do you have any info on that one?'

'What kind of boat are we talking about, sir.'

'I'm no expert on such matters but I can take a photo of it and send it to you?'

'Okay, here's my e-mail......I'll hold on.'

Rory pointed his phone camera at the boat and took two snaps one from the front and one side on. Then he sent it on.

'Just what I suspected. It's a 21' x 8' aluminium Work Boat powered by Volvo Penta. It's definitely an Oban boat. One of the missing of the three Volvo Pentas. No not missing, stolen of course.'

'That should be one happy owner, any day now.'

'So where is the Glad Tidings based now?' asked a very contented Rory with the progress being made.

'Glad Tidings is the name of several fishing boats around the British coast but Glad Tidings as a Volvo Penta? No sighting I'm afraid. This is a sure unregistered drug-runner you've got here, Sergeant.'

'Yes, valuable evidence.'

'I'll send a report on our discussion and findings. That might suffice as a production. If it is, I hopefully won't be needed as a witness in Ayr sheriff court.

'Early days, my friend. Not sure of the future timescale.'

Rory took a large open-mouthed yawn. It had been a long day. He demarcated the tied-up boat with police tape. Then he looked at his watch. It was approaching 5:20 am. Time to get home and a few hours sleep.

11

Later that morning, Rory was bright-eyed and coffee refreshed as he entered the interview room at Lamlash Police station.

'It's is 11:15 and I am interviewing Alexandru Dobrescu at Lamlash Police station. Also in the room is Constable Heather Blane.

Mr. Dobrescu, tell me in your own words what you were doing earlier this morning when you were arrested.'

Alexandru must have thought through his best option. There seemed little point in denying a dark sailing and being found with drugs. He could of course limit his part in the crime and that was in his mind when he chose to come clean.

'I bring drugs to Blackwaterfoot.'

'Why Blackwaterfoot?'

'It's is quiet especially early in the morning.'

'Where do you collect the drugs?

'I do not know.'

'You say you do not know but you bring drugs to Blackwaterfoot,' Rory said raising his voice.

'Please I try to help you,' Mr. Dobrescu said with pleading eyes.

'What does your colleague do?'

'My colleague? I no understand.'

'Yes, Marku Felea. He sails with you.'

Alexandru nodded without saying anything.

'What does Marku do?'

'He gives the bag to a man at the back of the Kinloch hotel.'

'You mean Mario Balan?' asked Rory.

'Yes, that be his name.'

Rory nodded retaining a happy outburst, excited to confirm Mario's activity. 'Your boat. The Glad Tidings. Where did it come from?'

'I do not know.'

'Alexandru, have you ever been to Oban?'

'Been where?'

'Been to Oban, a town on the seaside in the northwest of Scotland?'

'No, I no be in that place.'

'Okay, Mr. Dobrescu. You will be taken over to Ayr sheriff court later today and detained until your trial. You will be given a lawyer to defend you and a translator if you wish. In our system, the sooner you accept your guilt the shorter the sentence, you understand? You have been very helpful today.'

'I go understand.'

'This interview terminated at 11:55 am.'

At 2 pm after a light lunch and a packet of vinegar crisps, and a power-nap of ten minutes, Rory was woken by a telephone call. It made him scratch his head and bang the table. Skipper Alexandru's mobile phone was old, cheap, and did not have a tracking device on its settings. He had not expected that. But he was ready to interview Mario Balan.

'It is 2.20 pm and I am interviewing Mario Balan. Constable Heather Blane is also in attendance.'

Rory placed his pad of paper on the secured table as Mario's eyes followed his every movement. 'Mario you were found receiving drugs now known to be cocaine. What happens to the cocaine after you receive it?'

'I no reply.'

'You made a statement to the police about Mr Ronnie Jackson. That was to get him out of the way of your drug operation wasn't it?'

'No reply.'

'What do you do with the drugs?'

'I can't tell you.'

'You must tell the court so you might as well start here.'

Rory left a moment for him to consider what he had said. It did move the case on, he was able to see.

'I take them to a Romanian man in Brodick.'

'Well, there aren't many. We'd soon identify him. Who is he?'

'He runs a newsagents shop in the village. Mr. Radu Petrescu.'

'Okay, that's enough for the time being. The interview ends at 14:43.'

'Can I go now?' asked Mario.

'Oh yes you can go but when we are ready. You are going on a big boat to Ayr,' said an honest but teasing Rory.

Rory spent almost the rest of the afternoon making a report to Helen at the fiscal's office in Ayr. He ended with the probability of another arrest. That prompted a reply.

'What, you telling me another arrest is likely? Does that mean a custody case too?'

'Probably, I'll keep you informed.'

'Oh, and what about Ronnie Jackson? Can he get back to Blackwaterfoot yet?'

'Yes, um...yes, there's a police cordon around the boat but he'll not interfere with that. Yup, he can come home at last.'

'Great news, our budget was beginning to struggle with the hotel bill.'

They laughed simultaneously then ended the call.

Moments later he lifted the phone and spoke to Hugh Boag, the editor at the Arran Banner. 'Hi, Hugh. I'm lifting the news embargo. This will be a big story.'

'Can I come and see you about it?'

'It will have to be tomorrow, Hugh. We're about to make another arrest.'

The police car with Rory and Constable Gordon Mearns on board set off from Lamlash heading for Brodick and Mr. Radu Petrescu's newsagents. When they approached the village centre, they parked just off the main road and by foot went to the shop.

As the two uniformed officers entered the shop Mr. Petrescu looked at them with the startled eyes of an owl. 'Mr. Petrescu, you are charged with possession and the supply of category A drugs namely cocaine. Please come with us.'

There was no escape from the shop or the island for that matter and he almost offered his wrists to be handcuffed even before he saw them being produced. He was seated as they made a cursory look around the shop. Then walking behind the counter, on a ledge underneath was a notebook. Rory lifted it and read a list of names to himself. He showed it to Mr. Petrescu. 'Newspaper clients or drug deliveries?'

'Newspapers of course,' he said defiantly. 'I am a newsagent.'

Rory flicked through some more pages. 'There seem to be a lot of customers on the mainland, Ayr, Saltcoats, Prestwick, Troon, Ardrossan, Glasgow.'

The city was also underlined. 'Now I know there are newsagents in these towns. I don't expect them to order their daily newspaper from Arran for one moment, do you?'

Mr. Petrescu looked at his feet then whispered. 'No, you're right, my cocaine customers.'

Sorry I didn't hear what you said,' whispered a silently pleased Rory.

'I said they are my cocaine customers.'

'Come on then. The car's outside. Let's have some questioning at Lamlash for you.'

'This interview commences at 3.55 pm. I am interviewing newsagent, Mr. Radu Petrescu, in the presence of constable Gordon Mearns. Can you give me your full name?'

'Radu Petrescu. I have no middle name.'

'And you are a newspaper seller in Brodick. How long have you been there?'

'I have been there for twelve years.'

'Do you know Mario Balan, Alexandru Dobrescu, and Marku Felea?'

'Yes, they are my relatives.'

'What all of them?' asked Rory in surprise.

'Yes, my mother married twice and so Mario, who is married to Elena Balan, is of the first marriage. Alexandru and Marku are my cousins.'

'Are you all legally entitled to be in the UK?'

'I am. I have a British passport now. The others have no papers. I bring them over for work but in Arran only seasonal work. I needed money to support them. So I get a list of people who need cocaine.'

Rory lifted his cocaine client's book. 'There are a lot of names and addresses. Are you saying they all get cocaine?'

'Yes, all of them'

In silence, Rory's finger searched for any familiar names or local Ayrshire drug dealers. His heart stopped for a moment. He left his finger on one name. He beckoned Gordon over to show him a name with his other hand. He saw it and looked at Rory. 'God, this will get to the front page.'

Their eyebrows heightened. They had just noticed client number 78 was Sheriff Mark Constance.

'It's 4.10 pm. The interview is terminated to allow Mr. Petrescu to get the boat to the mainland and police custody at Ayr.'

No sooner had Mr. Petrescu left Lamlash police station, than Rory was on the phone to Helen.

'Hi, Helen. Are you busy?'

'Well, if it's important, please let me know.'

'Big fish here. An arrest for the Troon police, I hope. A supply of cocaine is arriving at 50 Fullarton Drive, Troon.'

'Okay, then you just pass it on to the Troon boys and if it's a custody case I'll hear from them. Happy with that?'

'No, wait. Do you know who lives there, do you?'

'Doesn't matter, does it?' she snapped back.

'It certainly does. That's the home of Sheriff Mark Constance.'

'What? You must be joking. Mark Constance? That will mean he'll have to leave the bench,' she said twiddling her fingers with the beads of her jade necklace with a smile as wide as the Firth of Clyde.

'And is that not a relief? Was that not worth a moment of your precious time,' he laughed.

12

Ronnie arrived home by taxi. He smiled all the way from Brodick as he felt welcomed home by the island of his birth. Thirty-five minutes later he was home to find his home was fusty. So he opened all the windows and left the front door open too. Everything was in place the way Elena had left it. He went to the fridge. It was empty. He filled the kettle and set it to boil but the plug was not in its socket. As he waited for the kettle to boil fruitlessly there was a call from the front door.

'Ronnie, are you there?' asked Ann the Home Help Advisor.

Ronnie returned to the hallway and saw a woman. He did not recognise Ann. He shut the door in her face.

She rang the bell. 'Ronnie I've brought some essentials for you. Some milk and cheese, bread and jam a couple of take-away meals too.'

The door opened.

'Do you remember me? I arranged for Elena to be your home help. Remember?'

Ronnie opened the door enough to let her enter.

'Now where will I put these things?'

'In the fridge,' he replied having seen the food.

'Then let me into the kitchen and I'll put the milk, margarine, cheese, and meals there but the jam and bread

I'll leave on the side.' She noticed the kettle switched on.

'Were you boiling water, Ronnie?'

'Yes, it will soon be ready.'

'No, it won't. At least not till I put the plug in the wall,' she advised him with a sympathetic smile. Then Ann came through to the lounge and sat on the couch. Ronnie remained standing.

'Well, you have been away for three months or so. You will be glad to be home.'

Ronnie sat down and Ann noticed his sombre mood.

'How are you feeling today, Ronnie?'

Ronnie's face turned towards Ann. 'I can't play billiards any more.'

'Did you play billiards in Kilmarnock?'

'I've not been to Kilmarnock for a long time,' he replied.

Ann took out her notepad and began to write.

'What are you writing?' Ronnie asked.

Ann looked up at Ronnie who seemed much older than when she last visited him to assess his ability to work with Elena.

'Ronnie, I feel it's time for you to go to a Care Home, you understand?'

'Is that another prison?'

'No, no it's a friendly place with residents of your own age......'

'Do any play billiards?'

'I don't know but I am sure that will be possible. There might even be a billiard table there to play on and make new friends.'

'Where is this?'

'I'm thinking about the Cooriedoon Care Home at Whiting Bay. Maybe you have heard about it? Do you think you would like that?'

'You will have to ask Helen, she finds nice places for me to stay.'

Ann wracked her brain. She just had to ask.

'And Ronnie, tell me who is Helen?'

'Helen works at court and put me in a hotel.'

Ann placed a big question mark on her page.

'What I'm going to do is have a big meeting with you, your GP, a health visitor and a staff member from Cooriedoon. Would you agree to attend?' she asked with a lump in her throat, feeling sorry for Ronnie's advancing dementia.

'Wow, lots of people. Perhaps some play billiards.'

'Perhaps some do. But not at the meeting. It's your chance to see if we can make your life a good bit easier,' she responded with more information for him.

'How?' asked a confused Ronnie.

'Well all your meals will be provided, you will enjoy the activities they have and there's a piano so you can have a sing-song at times. Sounds good, doesn't it?'

'Yes, I'd like that,' he smiled graciously.

'Good. So I'll be off now and get that ready for you.'

'Yes, it's time I got back to work again.'

'Oh, what were you doing before I arrived.'

'I can't remember. But I must go now; I don't want to be late.'

'Late for what?' she asked surprised. 'Where are you going Ronnie?'

Then he remembered. 'I'm a postman. That's what I do.'

Sheriff Mark Constance put up a solid defence at his Sheriff's tribunal. Cocaine was an upper-class recreational drug that he was addicted to, he told his professional tribunal. It did not affect his work as a sheriff, he maintained. He told the bench of fellow sheriffs that London was awash with cocaine and so many senior police officers indulged that no prosecutions are brought. It's the drug of celebrities. It should not be an A classified drug. As to his supply, he knew the drugs came from Arran and it seemed right that the middlemen were hard-working honest men supplying a genuine need. His supplier he said ran a business in Brodick. How else could he get a regular supply of happiness? To make matters worse, he begged his fellow sheriffs to try cocaine for its efficacious effects.

But when his defence ran dry, his sheriff brothers by majority decided to strike him off the bench and force his early retirement. It was inconceivable for him to deal with any drug cases fairly ever again. It was not a unanimous vote but a sizeable one nevertheless. It did cloud over the suspicion that two other sheriffs might find themselves in Mark Constance's shoes before too long. A final reminder to Mark came from the chairman of the disciplinary board. It was a reminder that he also faced a charge which will lead to a court appearance.

And it did. On a dreich, miserable, low clouded November 2nd Sheriff Mark Constance was found guilty of possession of the controlled drug cocaine and supplying it to several individuals in Troon.

Sheriff Principal A D Martin took the case in Glasgow and Constance was sentenced to four years at Kilmarnock Prison. He became the centre of attention in jail, the butt of many court jokes as well as barbed comments were made about the case of innocent dementia sufferer Ronnie Jackson.

12

Ronnie visited the Cooriedoon Care Home at Whiting Bay and found himself at home immediately. He enjoyed a sumptuous lunch in the company of what seemed to be contemporaries and to his delight was told that a billiard table would be identified as a priority fund-raising future activity. He was taken around the building and he saw a well cared for garden which delighted him. He began to study the flora, looking especially for chrysanthemums. Then his eyes were lowered as he inspected the lawn.

'Are you all right?' his guide, Mandy, enquired.

'You have no moss in the lawn. No weeds for me to pull. I don't think there's much for me to do in the garden.'

'It is a garden for you to enjoy; walk round, sit with an afternoon cup of tea, talk to residents,' Mandy said.

'Residents?' queried Ronnie looking vaguely to the clouds. 'Are any of them not guilty like me?' he enquired.

Mandy thought for a moment but was used to speaking to residents with dementia and puzzling minds. 'All our residents are innocent. This is not a prison,' she told him with a pat on his arm.

Ronnie took what she said on board for a brief moment. 'Kilmarnock was a good prison. I liked it there. It had a billiard table.'

'That's right Ronnie,' she said taking the conversation no further.

'I'll have to get up very, very early if I stayed here.'

'And why would that be?' she asked him taking his arm.

'Because, I am a postman,' he said looking out of focus beyond the road.

Skipper Alexandru Dobrescu was willing to talk. He had been detained pending trial at Kilmarnock prison and Rory had travelled there to continue his investigation.

'Alexandru, you will help yourself if you can answer my questions truthfully,' Rory began with a smile towards him and his Romanian accused skipper smiled back.'

'The drugs. Where did they come from?'

'I collected them at a small bay near Saddell, on the Mull of Kintyre.'

Rory's Dictaphone was inched forward instinctively as Rory felt a full confession was possible.

'How regularly?'

'Usually twice a week mid-week when we thought it would be quiet at Blackwaterfoot. We always brought small amounts, just in case we got caught.'

'And where did the cocaine come from before you collected it?'

'A van brought it from Machrihanish.'

'Machrihanish? asked Rory with his eyebrows reaching his forelocks. That's a very small town. They can't store many drugs in such a community, surely.'

'They store them on Rathlin Island in Northern Ireland.'

'What? But that's an inhabited island.'

'No, but there are fewer than 100 people and some of them help to store the drugs from Columbia.'

'Wait a minute, how do they come from Columbia?'

'That's where quality cocaine comes from. But they come to Rathlin Island from Iceland.'

Rory scratched his head. He had only got to the snake's tail and its head seemed a long way off. He felt out of his depth with the international dimension of the interview but it had to be completed and sent to the appropriate Police Scotland office.

'So how did you get involved with this?'

'I came from Romania to Scotland four years ago. I could not find work. I lived in Glasgow at the time. I remember going to Sammy Dow's pub in Shawlands, on the south side of the city. That was where I met Sharky Brown. He told me he could find good work for me. That was when I heard about the cocaine from Iceland and how it arrived on Rathlin Island. He said he'd get a boat as he knew I told him I used to sail on the Bucura Lake in Romania.'

'Sharky Brown. What do you know about him?'

'He lives in Glasgow and Radu sends him packets and boxes of cocaine. I haven't spoken to him for a long time.'

'And Mario, how did he get involved?'

'Mario, how do you say, is an illegal. He was in need of money. He work as odd-job man at the Kinloch hotel. He come to the island as he had a relative in Brodick. His wife was a home help. He agreed to forward the drugs to Radu Petrescu the newsagents in Brodick and send the boxes of cocaine by post to Sharky in Glasgow as well.'

Rory sat back and smiled at Alexandru. 'I see how you got involved and the others are fitting into place. I can't say how your case will go but if you tell the court in Ayr and in time in Glasgow for Sharky, what you are telling me, it might be able to shorten your sentence.'

Rory ended the interview a contented man but there was still much work to be done. He telephoned his colleague in the serious crime department in Glasgow and learned Sharky Brown was known to them. They would welcome Alexandru's statement as soon as possible to put Sharky Brown and his evil ways, behind bars, once more. Sharky was a big fish indeed.

But to get to the hub of this international drug-running case, planning meetings took place in Glasgow with police from Northern Ireland and Iceland too.

Marku Felea was given three years for his part in trafficking drugs from Saddle to Blackwaterfoot, and then he was deported. Skipper Alexandru Dobrescu received two years in prison and became the Crown's witness in Glasgow and Ayr, after which he too was deported back to Romania.

Mario received three years and was then also deported back to Romania to join his wife Elena, who left Scotland immediately, as she was an illegal immigrant.

In the Glasgow High Court, Lord Gavin Peacock sentenced Sharky Brown to eight year's imprisonment, as the mastermind behind the drug running in the west of Scotland and for the theft of Skylark II from the harbour at Oban.

In Kilmarnock Prison, Alexandru met Sheriff Mark Constance. The latter began to learn Romanian, a Latin-Romance language and Alexandru became a very competent Bridge player with the erstwhile Sheriff. Mr. Constance was quick to drop his title to fit in more readily. The Law Society of Scotland had already stripped him from their ranks.

Ronnie settled in the Cooriedoon Care Home with ease. He was able to wander around the home and was often found in the kitchen offering a hand to prepare meals. His wanderings outside the home were restricted for his safety. After one early morning, he was found on the road heading south for Lagg at 4 am. Once a postman, always a...

His billiards began to fade in his mind but ten pins carpet bowling caught his attention at the care home. He enjoyed the company of staff, community sing-songs, and the many visitors of relatives, of entertainers, and of service providers. In time his new lifestyle pattern meant rising later. 6 am was still early but his days of beach walking at 4 am were over.

On the 2nd of April the following year, the Chief Constable of Scotland arrived at Cooriedoon and presented Ronnie with a plaque. It was to celebrate Ronnie's initiative in reporting what he saw, which led to the successful prosecution of some 32 drug dealers in the UK, Iceland, and Northern Ireland. It was a significant case reminded the Chief Constable and a very satisfying outcome had come about, thanks to Ronnie.

And Ronnie was the centre of attention as a cake appeared with his name on it in red, white, and blue icing with a marzipan border too. After hearing the praises heaped on him by the Chief Constable, Ronnie was asked to say a few words. He was pleased to do so.

'Ladies, and ladies and gentlemen. I have enjoyed being a postman. It is very good of you to show your appreciation for all the homes I have visited and the walking I have done in the process for many years. I am still a very happy postman now and will bring your letters to you, now that I am in Lamlash. Thank you.'

He hesitated as did his audience. They felt short-changed. There was some who smiled graciously at him while others seemed bemused. He felt he had said enough. But one thing was now on his mind. 'Now, where did I put that glass down?' he said agitated for a moment. Then the Chief Constable led the applause. Ronnie looked around to see hands clapping and he started to clap too, although not sure why. That action started another round of applause and eventually, Ronnie remembered he had given a speech and he bowed not once, but six times.

The End

Interview With The Author

Police cells and Prison. You speak with authority. How and Why?

I have been in many prisons; firstly as the writer in residence at the Scottish Prison Service at Dumfries; I undertook a study tour of Canadian prisons through the Scottish Association for the Study of Offending of which I have been its chairman; Police station cell visitation and Prison visitation too. I was also the regional reporter to the Children's Hearings which meant I had to prosecute children who denied the ground for referral, in the sheriff courts at Kilmarnock, Ayr, and Dumfries. I have also given evidence in the County Court at Chelmsford. And finally, I have toured several prisons in both England and Scotland with my musical friend Dave Benrexi (on YouTube) playing his songs to detainees. I am therefore aware of many penal establishments in the land and their procedures.

A Second Arran Book. Will there be more?

These Arran books are my first trilogy of books. None were easy to write but the size of Arran, its communities, geography, and spirit of welcome, possessed me. I have enjoyed holidays at Blackwaterfoot but feel the happenings going on in that community need a rest or Blackwaterfoot will be seen by some as the country's leading crime scene. Nothing could be further from the truth. But, for the time being, no more Blackwaterfoot tales. Perhaps I should turn my attention to the east coast of the island next.

50 Fullarton Drive Troon. Did a sheriff really live there?

No, I lived there before coming to Dumfries.

Did you always want to write books?

This will be my 28th book and it seems I was destined to write. Perhaps because I grew up in a manse where my father would lock himself away on a Friday night and churn out sermons. Over a lifetime, he would have been able to compile many books. In fact, he only wrote one; *Poet's Progeny* about our family's link to Robert Burns. But as a student I always scored well in my essays and in my work as the regional then first authority reporter to the children's panels, I had to write reports until I took ill and retired. What could I do? So I began writing books.

What will your next book be?

I had a dream. In fact, I have many dreams. Then I thought if I asked a few friends if they had dreams, it might become a book. And so was born *The Dream Net*. It is a most unusual book. Not just because it has no chapters but the contributions come from Illinois, The Netherlands, Kyrgyzstan, Australia, Romania, Serbia, Eire, all parts of the UK, Vermont and Massachusetts.

ACKNOWLEDGEMENTS

Retired Constable Martin Greenlees was invaluable in showing me how the police plan a major incident. Martin is the author of the *Community Cop Colin* series. Constable Jane Dunbar also gave further advice on police initiatives. My thanks go to both of them. Thanks too to daughter Fiona, procurator fiscal, who confirmed legal procedure. Much appreciation goes to both M J Steel Collins my editor and publisher and Mathilde Vuillermoz my film agent who encourages my efforts. To Hugh Boag, editor of the Arran Banner, who has provided local interest in the Blackwaterfoot trilogy, many thanks, Hugh. My penultimate gratitude goes to the long-suffering residents of Blackwaterfoot who deserve a mention too. They can relax now. The action is over. Retain your rural character where very little of consequence happens. Yet without their village, there would be no trilogy of Blackwaterfoot stories. Finally, thanks to my software developer wife who gives me time to walk the dog, shop, cook, and iron, activities all of which allow my mind to wander and be creative.

SEAWEED IN HER HAIR

MILLER CALDWELL

Copyright

Dedicated to my beautiful and clever daughters,
Fiona and Laura

1

17 Huxley Gardens was their first home. A leafy suburb was the description on the Estate Agent's brochure but the heavy hum of the traffic on the North Circular Road and the groans of rising aircraft from Heathrow niggled on Kate and Greg's minds. A move on, as soon as they could, was constantly in her thoughts. They were thoughts not as prominent in Greg's life.

Kate travelled into the City each morning as a hair stylist at Nuthatch in the fashionable Chelsea district. It meant leaving the house to the grating sound of gurgling rooks at 6:30 am each morning. Greg left an hour later when the constant gear changing, tyre screeching and exhaust belching of cars filled his ears and nose as he made for the busy bus stop. There were usually eight awaiting the bus with a ninth passenger always late. One traveller usually delayed the driver, until he arrived out of breath and jumped onto the bus. Despite this activity, no word was ever spoken. Not even a nod of appreciation from the breathless passenger was seen while those already seated turned their heads away with frowning faces and buried their eyes in their morning paper.

Five stops later, Greg alighted from the bus and walked a further two hundred yards aware that cars at the pavement parked space-less. Like dominoes in a straight line. The morning sun burned in a sky of marvellous blue serenity making the drooping leaves of the trees shine brilliant and the pale blossoms expand to their fullest beauty.

Most of Greg's clients were office workers, retired couples, and unmarried youngsters hoping their work-outs would keep their bodies in shape. The Body Perfect was owned by Greg. An inheritance at his mother's death two years before along with a considerable sum from his unmarried god-father funded his venture. His heart was in his business providing a personal service to clients and managing a staff of three, enthusiastic in offering several demanding routines. His lead Yoga teacher walked into his studio last year. She was from the foothills of the Himalayas and had practiced Yoga all her life. Accordingly, there were classes in Hot, Ashtanga, Bikram, and Moksha Yoga as well as Pilates and Spins. Male attendees often did push-ups with weights or trained like boxers with skipping ropes. Some sessions had quiet soothing music while at other times a heavy rock beat was heard to work-outs when the younger generation took to the floor.

Greg's home clients were at the Orchard Braes care home where he gave classes to stretch tired limbs, dance with the able-bodied, and sing songs accompanied by his guitar. It was a lifestyle which he enjoyed and Kate was equally happy receiving good tips from her wealthy clients and making bold hairstyles for her demanding sitters.

At the weekend, Kate worked a half-day while Greg had a full Saturday shaping and exercising bodies. It meant Sundays were the only real time they had together. A long lie-in was the start of their unwinding Sunday. Sunday Love Songs on Radio 2 woke them and a cup of tea brought them to life.

'Darling, in ten years, where do you see us?' asked Kate.

Greg stretched his arms above his head.

'Depends.'

Kate looked at him. 'Depends on what?'

'Depends if our Premium Bonds come up a winner; if either of us has an incapacitating illness, if we have a large family...if...hey what are you doing?'

Greg's question required no answer. Kate was pulling off his pyjama trousers.

2

A Pittshanger Lane park bench was where they sat watching couples pass by, later that lazy Sunday. The noise of playful children rang in their ears and two spaniels barked while a pair of Bernese Mountain dogs walked stately alongside their owners, dribbling saliva as that breed are prone to do. The gentle sound of tennis balls pinged back and forth on the nearby courts, made Greg count the rallies. Some were odd, others even.

'Penny for your thoughts,' asked Kate.

Greg smiled and peered over his sunglasses. 'Nothing really. Well, counting tennis balls, I suppose.'

Kate laughed. She turned to look at her husband of six years. 'I asked you last night about our future. Remember?'

'Yeah, our future. In ten years? I have no idea. There's no point seeing that far into the future. You can't do anything about it, I mean, can you?'

Kate stood up, turned round, and took Greg's hand. 'Come, let's walk around the park.'

They joined the impromptu procession wheeling prams and dogs around the path.

'Well, I don't see myself here in ten years,' she said.

'Okay, where will you be?'

'Somewhere quieter. Wilder perhaps. Where life is slower and people talk to one another.'

'It's all in an ideal world, isn't it? I mean yes, we'd all like to live on a deserted island....with nine gramophone records...a book....a luxury item ...'

'Not nine. You'd only get a choice of eight records.'

Greg nodded acknowledging his error. 'So you are on your own? Where am I?'

'It's more than a dream. I'm talking reality. I can always style hair and you can still run a fitness club. Our work is transferable. We could go anywhere.'

Greg did not answer. He did not want to sound too optimistic and anyway he was distracted by a girl in a bikini on the grass. An upheaval was being proposed, with no real plan. It was a non-starter in his mind. Change was something this Londoner did not take kindly. Kate did not continue the conversation but followed Greg's eyes.

'You men are all the same,' she said digging her fist into his ribs.

'It's the way we're made. Eyes seem to have to see such delights.'

'You won't see so many if we settle on an island, somewhere remote,' suggested Kate.

'You mean, like the Isle of Wight?'

'Remote I said, perhaps somewhere Scottish.'

Greg folded his arms. He seemed to be looking over the trees, in deep thought. 'Isle of Wight's not too far away from London.'

Kate sighed. 'The Isle of Wight is not far enough away. You can see the south coast clearly from the island. It's busy. The ferry is non-stop. I mean somewhere away from the southeast. It's sinking with millions of people. It's not where to bring up a family,' she said biting her lower lip.

Greg looked at Kate straight in her eyes. 'What about Lundy Island?'

'Lundy? Are you serious? How could we survive a week let alone a winter? It's practically uninhabited. There can only be a couple of dozen people on the island and they won't need a haircut very often and none of them would want a fitness regime. Keeping alive would be the fitness task on their minds.'

'Well, it was only a thought. No need to raise your voice. Lundy was at least quieter than the Isle of Wight,' said Greg kicking a pebble off the path.

The following Tuesday Kate was shampooing a Middle Eastern customer. Amal Zaidi was Egyptian and her hair was rich black and long. Kate found her a pleasure to work with and she told her so.

'In my country, mother's cut their daughter's hair. Daughters cut their grandmother's hair and so everyone has their hair cut. There are Barber's shops where the men go to have their hair, moustaches, and beards trimmed but women are not allowed in.'

'Your English is very good, Amal.'

She smiled at Kate. She tapped her on her wrist. 'It should be. I was schooled in London and my husband has been here for the past fifty-four years.'

'I don't think I could work in the city for the next ten years,' she said to her new audience.

'My dear, then I'd miss you.'

'Oh, there are some very good hair stylists around. I'd soon be replaced,' Kate said with a whalebone brush in her hand.

'You are being serious. Where were you thinking of going?'

'We haven't decided yet. I thought an island. Not too big but not too small, somewhere in Britain.'

'Would you consider Scotland?' Amal asked looking in the mirror to asses her response.

'Well yes, I suppose so, but the weather..err..'

'God provides rain because the land and its people need water. But you might be surprised; some islands like Arran have wonderful summers and pleasantly mild winters. You should consider Arran.'

'Aran is that not an Irish Island?'

Amal laughed. 'Forgive me laughing. Aran with one 'r' is in Ireland but Arran with two is in the Firth of Clyde.'

'I'll have to investigate that one,' she replied thinking Amal knew the country better than she did and it sounded ideal. A Scottish island not too far north in Scotland.

'Well, I can tell you it has a population of four and a half thousand residents with just as many visiting throughout the year.'

A puzzled expression took hold of Kate's face. 'But how do you know such facts about Arran?'

'My husband owned a holiday cottage with a trout beat on the island until two years ago. We sold it.'

'Why sell it? Were you unhappy?'

Amal laughed once more. 'Do you know how old I am?'

Kate shook her head with a puzzled look.

'I will be seventy-six next year and my husband is eighty-three. It was time to sell. He is no longer fishing or walking so much. But yes, I'm sure you would like Arran. Do give it some thought. Go visit it first. It will be a significant decision but I'm sure you will love it.'

Kate smiled at her. 'Your hair is dry, let me remove the dryer.'

'Thank you. You must have hope, as I do,' she giggled.

Kate smiled as she brushed any lingering hair from Madame's shoulders.

'My name is Amal, as you know. It means "to have hope". And you must have hope too.'

Greg returned home that night as the rice in the pan was being drained. Two dinner plates were prepared to receive the curry. He entered the kitchen and pecked his wife on her cheek. 'An atlas in the kitchen?' he approached the open book and lifted it.

'Bloody Scotland,' he said in a voice loud enough to be heard, then closed the atlas.

The next Friday night it was Greg and Kate's turn to invite her sister Lizzie and her husband, Alan, over for an evening meal. Once a month they would have an evening turnabout to host each other. A month seemed the right time-lapse to catch up on their lives. That night during the second course of chicken Korma with poppadoms, the subject of Arran came up.

'Sounds great to me. That is if you have thought it through,' said the practical if not pedantic Alan.

'So, a new holiday venue for you too then, Alan? I see where you are coming from,' Greg said without a smile.

'Bit harsh there Greg,' said his wife giving him a sharp look.

'Quite a change it would be. Starting all over again. New friends, new home, lost old friends...' said Alan.

'Not these days, Zoom, Skype, Face Time we'll keep in touch. No problem. Go with your gut feelings,' said Lizzie joining in the debate.

Kate gathered the plates. 'I guess I'm keener than Greg,' she said as she made her way to the kitchen, with plates piled high.

'You have transferable skills. You guys are lucky in that respect,' said Alan.

Greg nodded. 'Probably easier for Kate. Experienced hairstylist, she'd soon get her clients. She's good at her job.'

'Costed it out?' asked Alan as Greg filled up the glasses with Beaujolais.

'Yeah, Alan, I'll sell this house and my business. Cheaper houses on sale on Arran, I'm sure, enough to get Kate set up. It would take me longer to take over a barn or something like that for a fitness studio,' he said unenthusiastically.

Kate arrived from the kitchen with a peach flambé then returned with a cartoon of ice cream.

'Mmm....this looks good,' said Lizzie.

'It will be plain eating on Arran. No baked Alaska I bet,' said Greg.

'Oh come on dear, it's not Timbuktu, surely? Five thousand people won't be eating spam every night.'

'Every other night, fish on the others,' said Greg smiling sarcastically.

Alan and Lizzie laughed somewhat nervously. They detected considerable reservation in what Greg was saying.

When Alan entered his home after their night out, he turned around and faced his wife.

'I can't see them going to Arran. Can you?'

Lizzie threw the car keys to him. 'Kate is up for it. Not sure about Greg.'

In bed that night Greg was tired. Kate was wide awake, sitting up.

'Then there's only one solution. Let's have a weekend on Arran, or perhaps a week, get a feel for the place, and then decide. Agreed?' She looked at Greg. He seemed to be considering her suggestion. But she was wrong. Greg rolled over and began to snore.

3

It was midsummer and they had managed to take a whole week off to visit Arran. They hired a Ford Kuga for the trip. The car's first stop was at the Keele service station on the M6. It was busy with cars seeming to leave as soon as others arrived. The hall area was shoulder-rubbing busy. They stopped at the Starbucks counter, ordered two coffees and two chocolate buns to go, and returned to their car.

'The air's much cooler up here and we're not yet halfway there,' said Greg.

'No, probably not halfway. But the air seems cleaner.'

'Anyway, if a week won't settle our future, we'll have to settle for London. We're not gallivanting around the country to find the ideal place if it doesn't exist,' Greg concluded.

Kate was getting irked by Greg's hesitations about Arran. She put her coffee down on the car's consul and turned her head towards him.

'Look here Greg. We're well on our way. There's no going back. So bloody well accept that and let's try and enjoy this break. If nothing else, I needed a break from work and I guess you do too.'

The silence lasted two minutes. Time for Greg to consider his feelings and appreciate what Kate was telling him. He felt trapped, like a fly in ointment struggling to rise up the side of the jar.

'You're right. I might as well enjoy this break. I've never been to Scotland.' Greg looked up at the sky. Striates of harmless clouds drifted by to the south making way for a darker and more hostile covering from the northwest.

By the time they were settling into a 70 mph cruise control speed, Greg was aware of two things. The traffic was thinning and the clouds were congregating and about to assault his car.

As the Cumbria county sign welcomed them on their northerly journey, the heavens opened. Greg dropped his speed to 50 mph and settled in the first lane, overtaking slower lorries on their way. As they passed Kendal the rain escalated, while the increasingly greasy front window wipers regularly waved away a steady drizzle sideways. The weather seemed to be settling in for some time.

'God stop, or you'll kill it,' shouted Kate all of a sudden.

Greg put his foot hard on his brake pedal as he looked in his rear mirror to check no one was behind him. But closing down on him was a transporter lorry. Greg indicated he was going into the emergency lane as the deer stopped in its tracks and then set off back from where it had come.

Kate screamed. Like the pull of a magnet, the deer froze in their path. The car with its lights on full hit the dazed deer at thirty miles an hour and seconds later they were gently shunted down the embankment from behind by the transporter.

Their car raced out of control down the outer embankment and stopped as it crashed into wire netting by the side of an A road running parallel to the motorway at a lower level. Silence ensued, broken only by the call of disturbed rooks. Fortunately, the car remained upright. Then a voice shouted.

'Are you alright?'

Greg thought he had asked that of his wife. He looked at her. She looked at him. They were alive.

'Hey, are you alright?' The sound was nearer this time. Then Greg heard a hand on his door and a man tugged it open.

'Hi, I was in the lorry behind you. I shunted you off the road. But....are you both okay...that's the main thing?'

'It could have been worse I suppose,' said a still dazed Greg.

'My arm hurts,' said Kate cradling her left arm with her right hand.

'Anywhere else? Any bleeding darling?'

'No Greg, I don't think so.'

Greg's head was bleeding. He undid his seatbelt and pushed the emergency bag out of the way.

'Looks like you'll be alright. I phoned the police and the ambulance service. They should be here soon,' said the relieved lorry man.

'What about this car?' asked Kate.

'The car?' said the lorry driver who then set off around it to see the damage. He returned and said, 'It's a write-off.'

'You sure?' asked Greg aware of its hired status.

'Trust me. I know about cars. The Kuga has a solid structure but it is not worth repairing. Scrap metal, that's what it is. Better get the car papers out before you leave here.'

It wasn't long before the faint sound of a siren was detected. The noise grew louder. The vehicle was not coming from the motorway but the A road in front of them. The blue flashing lights were perched on top of the vehicle and soon they saw an ambulance arrive. The ambulance parked on the other side of the fence. Two doors opened and closed.

'Be with you in a second,' shouted one ambulance man as the other brought out large wire cutters and started cutting the fence, creating an entrance to the crash site. Then they approached carrying two stretchers.

'Okay, I'm Pat. Let's see what we have here,' he asked as he shone a pen light into Kate's face. 'And what's your name?'

'I'm...Kate,' she struggled to inform him because of her pain.

'It's my arm that hurts and my neck is a bit sore as well.'

'I know. I see how you are holding your arm. It's almost certainly broken. You are likely to have whiplash too.'

'Hi, I'm Sue. Where is the pain, sir?'

Greg turned his head towards her. He lifted his hand to his head.

'I see, you've gashed your head. And what's your name?'

'Greg.'

'No back injury?

'No, I think I'm fine there.'

'Alright, it's not warm. Best get you in the ambulance and get you both checked out.'

'Where?' asked Greg.

'Westmorland General Hospital or the Penrith hospital. We're fractionally nearer the Penrith hospital. Hey Pat, Penrith?' he asked for clarification.

'Penrith to be sure,' Pat replied and Kate was aware for the first time of a Northern Irish accent.

Friday night at A&E Penrith had the usual falls and fights, the overdosed and the alcohol-fuelled arguments. But both Kate and Greg had been given an analgesic to ease pain and they lay still on beds awaiting attention.

Very soon thereafter, Kate was taken away, examined by the doctor then wheeled to the X-ray department.

Greg had a longer examination and was then sent for a CAT scan.

By 10 pm that night Kate was sitting up in bed with her arm in plaster. She had whiplash and been given an NHS folded sheet of paper asking her to walk around normally when discharged. "Movement aids whiplash healing," it stated. "Only return to the hospital if the pain gets much worse."

Greg returned half an hour later announcing that they could be released in 24 hours subject to a good night's sleep. His CAT scan revealed no injury and his bandaged head was all he could show for his mishap. They both sighed loudly relieved, at how fortunate they had been.

Greg took out his mobile and phoned the car rental firm. He explained what had happened and was told the police report will be sent to the company. The rental firm asked their state of health and Greg was informed that when he and Kate were free to leave the hospital, they were to get in touch and a car from the Kendal garage would be given to them to complete their journey.

Greg was pleased that their future seemed clearer and he told Kate. All that was missing was a hot mug of cocoa and sound sleep, thought Greg.

Footsteps were heard approaching. They entered the two-bed room.

'Good evening,' said the taller of the two police officers. 'Sergeant Ian Fox and Constable Margaret Nicolson. Mr. and Mrs. Bailey?'

Kate nodded. Greg confirmed their identity.

'Here are your car papers,' said Sergeant Fox as he laid them on the wooden side table.

'Oh thank you. I had forgotten to take them,' said Greg.

'As part of the enquiry, we'll need to interview you both. We've cleared it with the hospital staff. Mr Bailey, we'll go to a private room for the interview. Are you ready?'

Greg looked at Kate who looked worried. Constable Nicolson left the room and summonsed a nurse who arrived promptly. She wheeled Greg's bed to a nearby characterless room.

'Tell us in your own words, Mr. Bailey, what happened on the M6?' asked Sergeant Fox.

Almost an hour later, Greg was returned to the room while Kate was wheeled out for her interview.

She was asked the same questions. 'Well, we were travelling along, at an acceptable rate,' she began. 'I mean we were in cruise control. It had been raining. I was first to spot the deer leave the hard shoulder and enter the first lane. I remember shouting to Greg to stop the car.'

'And did he?' asked Constable Nicolson.

'No, not completely but he did slow down considerably.'

'Can you tell us how fast he was going?'

'Well, until the deer appeared we must have been doing 50-60 mph. It was very wet. The motorway wasn't very busy. Then after I shouted, Greg slowed down. Maybe 30 mph it was. It seemed straight away.'

'Unlikely. Probably nearer 40, I would think,' said Sergeant Fox.

'Then what happened?' asked Constable Nicolson.

Kate shuffled in her bed.

'You comfortable?' asked PC Nicolson.

'Yes, I suppose so,' she replied with a sigh. 'Err, you were asking what happened next. It was over in a flash really. We went onto the hard shoulder and so did the deer. The deer must have been transfixed by our lights. It did not move. Then we hit it. What a thud. Just as well it did not have horns. It brought us nearly to a stop. I mean we jolted forward a bit. That was the last I saw of the deer. It must have been a second later we got hit from the rear and that launched us off down the embankment. Launched is perhaps the wrong word. It was more of a shove forward.'

'Did you encounter the driver?'

'Oh yes, he came down to see if we were all right. He phoned for the emergency services too. I don't know what we would have done without him.'

'Did he smell of drink?'

'Good heavens no. His job was a lorry driver, I mean, he wouldn't would he?'

Constable Nicolson was scribbling in her diary, non-stop.

'How near was the lorry before it hit your car?' asked Sergeant Fox.

'Well, I don't really know. But he must have seen the deer too. He was sitting much higher on the road. I suppose he could have overtaken us but we might have overtaken the deer as well. I presume that is why he braked onto the hard shoulder too. I don't blame him. Would you? I mean what would you have done in the circumstances?'

The officers were taken aback by her question. 'I don't really know. It must have been instinct to take these dangerous decisions,' said Nicolson.

'So, what happens next?' asked Kate with white knuckles on show. She felt her heart beat audibly to the police.

'We complete our report, this one, your husbands and the lorry driver's statements. Then we'll have the road markings of course, and we submit all these to the Crown Office for their consideration,' said Fox familiar with the procedures.

'Will the Crown Office prosecute us?'

'I can't say. Depends on how they see it. But they have lawyers who look at health and safety issues as well.'

'Health and safety? Why?' asked Kate in a confused state.

'They look at how often accidents happen at that spot, consider adding more deer warnings, mandatory lowering of speeds where the accident happened, lots of things really.'

'But that does involve us. That's not about prosecution.'

'No it's not,' said Nicolson. 'But we really can't second guess the Crown Office's decisions, can we?'

4

Another Ford Kuga, this time a grey one, rested in the hospital car park. Kate walked slowly to the man by the car, aware of her niggling whiplash injury.

'Here are your keys and car papers sir,' said the smartly dark-suited, car deliverer.

'I'm dreadfully sorry about this,' said Greg looking suitably and sincerely contrite.

'Not to worry, sir. Accidents do happen. You are not the first,' he replied with a reassuringly broad smile.

'Yes, but the car is a write-off,' commented Greg.

'Not really. We get scrap metal out of it as well as spares. So, not really a complete write-off. Yes, better if any accident didn't happen. But that's not realistic. Have a pleasant journey Sir, Madam.'

'But can't we give you a lift back to your garage?'

The car deliverer pointed to a Jaguar sitting nearby. The driver was seated at the wheel. 'I've got my lift back, thanks.'

Greg was soon on the motorway again. This time cruise control was at 60 mph and both of them were slightly slouched forward. They were on the lookout for revengeful deer.

Half an hour later as they drove under a pass-over, they saw the welcome to Scotland sign and they immediately left the motorway for the west coast. However, there was still a long way away to go and the road took them on the Dumfries bypass half an hour later. Kate consulted the roadmap and saw the winding road up through Dumfries and Galloway to Ayrshire.

'Oh God, the Arran sailing. Our tickets were for yesterday,' said Greg gripping the steering wheel and looking like a frightened hare.

'Too late. Even if we have to spend an extra night in Ardrossan, we'll sort it out,' said Kate calming his fears.

'What else can go wrong,' said a grim-faced Greg.

'Let me phone the Ardrossan number. Now, where is it?'

Kate opened the glove box and found the correct papers and telephone number.

'Hello? Hi, we are Kate and Greg Bailey. We should have been on the ferry yesterday but, well,.... well we couldn't make it. Can you put us on sailing this afternoon instead?' she asked crossing her fingers on her uninjured hand.

'Now let me see. First, can you make the 2 pm or the 5 pm sailing?'

'I don't know,' she said biting her bottom lip.

'Well, where are you now?'

'Greg where are we now?' she asked placing her hand over her mobile.

'Almost at Kilmarnock.'

'Just about at Kilmarnock,' she informed him.

'If you don't make any stops I can get you onto the 2 pm ferry. Make sure you don't go into Kilmarnock. Take the exits, lots of roundabouts to go but you will soon see the boat symbol on signposts. Right, I'll book you on the 2 pm ferry. I've got your car registration details from yesterday. And it's the two of you, yes?'

'Err... no. We have a different car registration number,' she said rifling through the collection of papers. 'Ah, here it is SE18 RND.'

'I see. Had an accident then?'

Kate was taken aback. 'Umm yes, not serious though,' she said minimising her injuries and conveniently forgetting the written-off car.

'You are not the first to have had an accident and missed the sailing, not by a long chalk. So, 1:30 here at Ardrossan and you'll be on the 2 pm sailing.'

'Thank you so much. You've put our minds at ease,' said Kate taking a sigh of relief as soon as she switched off.

They passed the turn off for Troon, then Irvine, and saw the sea for the first time. The 'sleeping warrior' capped the Arran Mountains and the guide book made reference to them.

'I can see Arran. It can't be far off the mainland,' said Kate taking out her sunglasses and positioning them on the bridge of her nose.

Saltcoats was bypassed and they travelled to the end of Ardrossan before turning onto the shore road where they first saw the MV Caledonian Isles in port. They joined the queue of cars after a brief stop at the kiosk checking the car registration and the number of passengers aboard the car.

They gingerly left the car and made for the toilets. En route, Greg took a deep breath of sea air. So did Kate. They were nearly on Arran and their dream was materialising.

The voyage was just a few minutes over an hour. During that time, they had lunch then a walk on deck. Their hair blew this way and that as they held on to the wooden rail barrier. They saw porpoises ahead ushering the ship to port and the bobbing heads of grey seals on the lookout for any scraps which the passengers might throw overboard. Seagulls were more numerous, boisterous, and charming passengers into throwing pieces of sandwiches to them.

'Sea air is good for the hair, you know, strengthens the strands. Wish I could import the air to Chelsea,' said a smiling Kate.

'Not very practical. Perhaps you could gather seaweed instead,' suggested Greg with a gesture of his hand, like an actor.

'Yes, seaweed in my hair. That's even better,' she told him clinging on to his other arm.

They docked at Brodick and made their way to the Belvedere Guest House on Alma Road which they had booked.

'Welcome, welcome. I was getting a wee bit worried but you've made it. Come away in,' said their host Mrs. McSkimming.

'Yes, I'm afraid we had a road accident and that put us back a day. I'm sorry, we should have contacted you earlier.'

'Oh dear me. So that's a recent plaster, dearie?'

Kate closed her lips tightly and nodded.

'And you sir. I see you've been in the wars too?'

'Nothing serious I assure you,' Greg admitted.

'Well, I think a cup of tea is what you need. I'll put the kettle on,' Mrs. McSkimming said leaving Kate to sit in the lounge and focus her eye on the bird feeder outside the window. Greg emptied the car and brought the bags into the hallway.

'While the pot is brewing, I'll take you to your rooms upstairs.'

They followed Mrs. McSkimming to the spacious bedroom which sat at the back of the house. A neatly mown lawn was surrounded by a border of lupines and wisteria, poppies and forget-me-not edging. Through an open window, bees could be heard on their trumpet seeking patrols.

'The window's a wee bittie open. I always think it freshens the room. Close it if you wish but perhaps leave it open at night. Just to keep you at the right sleeping temperature. Well, I'll leave you to sort out your things. Come down as soon as you are ready, the tea will be too,' she laughed nervously and made her way downstairs.

Kate drew Greg to herself. She put her hand around his waist and stood on tiptoes to kiss him. 'She's really cute. I'm sure we have found a good base to explore tomorrow.'

'Okay, I hear you.'

They slept well and were woken by the smell of sizzling bacon, in the morning. Kate drew back the curtain and was assaulted by a sharp shaft of light. It was a cloudless sky. They would have cause for a spring in their step this day.

Their ablutions complete and the car with a full tank, they set off north on the east coast. There were a few villages to encounter and some like Sannox which came up too quickly, made them pass by without a stop but at Lochranza, there was time to park and explore.

They took the path through the golf course and saw deer once more but this time sitting on the greens and fairways of the course. They seemed so docile. Kate had a tear in her eye when recalling the fate of the last deer to confront her, a mere twenty-four hours ago. They looked at her as they passed. It seemed they knew one of their clan had been killed by the twosome. Such was their stare.

An enterprising coffee shop appeared as they started to walk up a soft incline. They decided to enter. It was mid-morning after all.

'Good morning, two coffees please.'

The woman looked at the pair, sizing them up. That'll be £2 with two cheese scones?'

'Oh rather, just the thing. Yes, two please.'

'Then that'll be £3.00 total.'

Kate handed over a five-pound English note.

'Keep the change,' she said as she smiled recognising the price paid, as paltry.

The woman raised the note to the light by the window. 'That's very kind of you,' the woman said.

'It's a real note,' said Kate smiling, having noticed her reticence in taking the money.

'I know it is. It's just that in England it's what they do to our Scottish notes. A bit of your own treatment, for fun, of course.'

Greg and Kate gave a forced pleasing grunt.

'Come from the London area, are we?'

'Yes as a matter of fact. We don't pay your prices in London, I can assure you.'

'I don't think they southerners are greedy. Just their overheads are so large. Rent and of course some well-heeled customers, I'm sure.'

'I agree. A rat race and wasn't it your Jimmy Reid who first talked about that? Rat races were for rats,' Greg replied sitting back in the hope all could appreciate his historical knowledge.

'So, on holiday?'

'Sort of,' said Kate sipping her hot coffee.

'Sort of?' enquired their host with a slanted head.

'With a view of living on the island,' Greg ventured.

The woman nodded silently for a moment. 'Well, what is it you do? I mean you are too young to retire.'

They both smiled. 'Greg runs a fitness gym in London. He wants to start one here,' said Kate rubbing Greg's knee in a moment of affection.

'A gym? Well, I guess you are trying to make us fit. We're a fit lot you know. The fishermen, the farmers, the community activities.'

'You mean there's no need for a fitness centre?' asked Greg feeling a little concerned while partly pleased.

'Don't get me wrong. There's a need for a gym. You'll have to get all those home exercise bikes and pull contraptions out of their garages. But you'll get enough to make ends meet. I guess. Especially in winter. And you, what do you do?'

'I'm a hairstylist,' said Kate.

'A hairdresser? Well, we've many shops around Brodick, Lamlash, even here at Lochranza,' the woman said.

'So a competitive market? Too many on the island,' Kate responded biting her bottom lip.

'No, not if you play your cards right. We're well catered for with hairdressers on the east coast. What we don't have are hairdressers a-plenty on the west coast. But there's no point getting a property converted into a salon, in the west,' she said shaking her head.

'Why,' asked Kate eager to find the elusive solution.

'Sparse population. Hamlets more than towns, all the way up and down. You'd make it if you had a mobile salon. Make it big time I reckon. Especially if you cut male heads too. They women would love that.....They have rough sea-blown hair and it needs regular shaping. Sea air makes the hair grow too, needs regular cutting as well. They would not have to have a day's outing to the east side of the island for a haircut. I think you've hit the nail on the head.'

Kate smiled at Greg. 'Looking good then, darling.'

Greg pouted his lips and nodded so minimally, it gave Kate an uncertain feeling.

The following day they left Brodick to see the west coast of the island. It was a changed day. A grey mist descended making tree lines disappear. The grey sea was white with angry waves and no horizon came into view. Greg struggled to keep his eye on the windy road, unfamiliar to him and challenging in the dampness.

Kate had a notepad on her lap to record as much information as possible, not trusting her memory. She cast her eyes on the silent Holy Island on their way south. The Buddhist sanctuary was only an outline in the mist.

'Mystical Island. We must visit that too,' she said.

'An island off an island, that's a bit too much. I'd never get work there.'

'Oh come on Greg, this is also a holiday, don't forget.'

'Forget? You are not driving.'

Kate said nothing, hoping Greg would get out of his negative thinking about their venture. She recalled all his recent comments since the accident. He did not seem himself. This was not the man she married six years ago. No seven years ago, by now. Seven. Was this the dreaded seven-year itch? Or was it something else?

5

From Dippen, the road left the shoreline and their focus changed to the forest on the right. The map showed a large wooded area and that meant no clients for either of them. But the rain seemed to be falling straight down on them, masking any civilization.

'No sign of any habitation. Just when I could do with a break,' he said.

Kate consulted her map. 'There's a hotel at Lagg, I think we should stop there.'

'Yeah, great. In fifty miles I suppose.'

'No Greg, only a few now. I'd say about four minutes ahead.'

'I'm counting.'

Despite it being mid-summer, there was a welcoming roaring fire in the hotel lounge's fireplace. Greg made straight for the loo. Kate took the opportunity to go too before they ate.

Seated on either side of the fire on the fender seat, they remained in silence until assistance arrived.

'Good morning, can I get you anything?' asked Pat the waitress.

'You say good morning. You haven't been outside have you?' asked a disgruntled Greg.

'Ah, the weather. It'll, clear up. It always does.'

'The same day?' asked Greg.

'Well that's a good question,' the waitress replied in a joyful manner, enjoying the banter.

'I'll have a coffee and a scone if you have them?'

She turned towards Kate and resumed her duties. 'Yes, madam we have scones, with cream and strawberry jam, cheese, or fruit?'

'What a choice. I'll have the cream and strawberry jam. Greg?'

'Black coffee. That's all.'

'Black coffee for you too, madam?'

'No, a white-flat if I may?'

'Certainly, they will be with you in a moment,' Pat said spinning round, making her skirt dance around her waist.

'What's wrong Greg?' She asked directly at him.

Greg lowered his head and fanned his palms in front of the fire. 'I get a feeling we are drawing apart. Don't you? I mean, you seem set on a new life here. I can't see the way forward for me.'

Kate wondered if that was all. She'd give him a chance to redeem himself. 'It's only our second day on Arran. Too soon to come to your conclusion,' she said bending towards him.

Greg stood up before the fire and warmed the seat of his trousers. 'It's more than that. I'm a city guy, always have been. Don't think I'll ever change.'

Kate was saddened by his expressed feelings. She felt trapped. Here on Arran, she felt a gentler pace with people ready to talk, with a healthy climate and fresh air, great sea views, and a great work opportunity. She tried but failed to reconcile her feelings with Greg's.

The atmosphere chilled despite the fire. Kate held her coffee in both hands. Her cream scone sat proudly on its plate, untouched. Greg moved away from the flames and looked out of the rear window onto the hotel's back garden. Lush bushes and border flowers stood like wet soldiers resenting their daily drill. Another couple passed through the lounge.

'Good morning, not a day to be outside,' said the jolly chap in his plus fours carrying a tweed deer stalker hat. His wife followed on, seemingly knowing her place. She giggled nervously. 'I hope the weather changes,' she managed to say as she left the room. Greg gave a weak smile, acknowledging their departure and glad of no more mindless talk.

'Let's go. Let's be on our way,' he said.

Kate scowled at him. 'I've still to eat my scone and drink my coffee. Now sit down and act less like a child,' she said sternly.

Greg did as he was told but looked as glum as the china pug staring at him from a corner of the room.

They resumed their journey with distrust in the air but Kate was not wishing to promote hostility. She consulted the map.

'Blackwaterfoot seems to be the largest village on this side of the island. We could explore it a bit.'

Greg was at a loss how the rest of the day would develop so a walk around the village sounded a better option.

'Okay,' was all he managed to say.

They took a sharp left turn to approach the village. As they made their way to the shore they realised it was more substantial than their map implied. A white-walled hotel appeared before them with a large car park. They entered it and with sparsely distributed vehicles, they were able to face the sea.

'Just look at that, Greg. Pure magic and look over there, a seal on a rock.'

'Where?'

'There,' she pointed.

'I guess they like this weather.'

Kate put her hand out of the window. 'It's dry. It's not raining. Come on, let's walk along the beach.'

They locked the car doors and set out along the road leading to the shore. Just before they got to the golf course, there was a row of private houses. The very last one had a sign on the lawn. It simply read For Sale.

Kate stopped and looked at the house. 'I wonder how much they are asking. Can we knock on their door?'

Greg put up no resistance as Kate rang the doorbell. She could hear a dog respond to her bell ringing. The door opened and a young woman of around twenty-eight years opened the door. She wore blue jeans and a light brown pullover supporting the chain of a good-luck necklace. Her shoes were house slippers.

'Do excuse our impromptu call but we see your home is for sale. Not so?'

'Yes, has been on the market for some time now, almost a year.'

'That's a long time,' said Greg.

'Yes, I don't live here usually. I work in Glasgow. My father died last year and my mother is now in a care home. She has Alzheimer's disease.'

'I'm sorry to hear that,' said Greg.

'That's why I am down here, to tidy up. Sorry, the house is still a bit dusty. Despite that, would you like to see around the house?'

'If it's convenient,' said Kate. And it certainly was.

'I'm Sue, Sue Parker.'

'I'm Kate and this is my husband Greg.'

They shook hands. 'Come in. Don't mind the dog, she's on her last legs and partly deaf. Now, this is the lounge, the main room downstairs.'

Kate and Greg's mouths were open as they took in the view over the sands and out to sea. A better view they could not imagine. In the bay window was a telescope on a tripod pointing to the sky above the horizon.

'Don't suppose the telescope goes with the price?' asked Greg optimistically.

'Oh yes, it does. If I had it in my flat in Gardner Street, I'd be reported for being a peeping Tom,' she laughed and so did the others.

'As children, we used to spy on yachts go by, see submarines at close range, see people playing golf on Kintyre and great for ornithology. It brings back many happy memories for me.'

'I'm sure you will have many happy memories of here.'

'Oh, and as it's a bay window, you get the sun from 3 pm until it's dark in this room.'

'Perfect,' said Kate smiling at Sue.

'The kitchen is at the back of the house. It gets the sun in the morning.' Then they were led to that room. Not only was the kitchen sunny, but the room was also spacious and had a dining table. The units seemed new.

'It looks like a magazine kitchen,' said Kate

'We had it gutted two years ago. It was meant to see my parents out, as it were, but as I told you, it didn't work out that way.'

There was a bedroom at the back of the house then they were taken upstairs where three bedrooms and the bathroom were situated. The back bedroom was spacious with views inland, unobstructed and they had a closer view of the rear garden lawn, in need of a cut. The rich dark soil supported a mass of varied flower colours.

'The soil is sandy as you can imagine. Dad was a keen gardener. He brought in tons of dark soil for the flower borders.'

Sue was in no rush to move them on and neither were Kate and Greg as they looked at the garden, the greenhouse, and the enclosed hedge. A morning suntrap was their conclusion. Neighbours were unseen and to all intents, unheard.

The bathroom was quite out of this world. A shower over a bath in one corner and a jacuzzi filled the other. The colours were cotton blue and white, once more a picture postcard.

'As you can see we have a jacuzzi in the bathroom but you were unable to see the hot tub in the back garden. It's on the patio near the back door.'

The two front bedrooms were spacious with deep enclosed storage space. The views being at the front were even more spectacular as they were raised above the lounge. And in the upstairs hallway, there was access to the rafters where there was additional storage space.

'Well, that's the house apart from the garage at the side of the house. It's totally empty now, that is apart from my car. Do you want to see it too, I mean the garage of course?' she sniggered at her ambiguity.

'I'd love to get the whole picture of the house in my mind. Yes, that includes the garage too,' said Greg.

As they made their way down and out past the hot tub to the garage, Sue needed to find out more about her prospective buyers.

'And may I ask, what line are you in?'

'I run a fitness studio in Fulham,' said Greg.

Sue gave a silent hum but did not respond further to him. 'And you Kate? Are you working?'

'At present, I am a hairstylist in Chelsea but I'm planning to run a mobile hair salon on the west coast of the island.'

'That should go well. Just what we need on this side,' she told her with a glint of reality, knowing she could never be a client of a Chelsea hairstylist in Glasgow.

'And how are you going to set up a fitness suite on Arran, Greg?' asked Sue.

Greg took a deep sigh. 'Well, it's not happening for me yet.'

Sue gave him a sympathetic smile. 'You'll have to set up on the east coast, where the population is. But a Fulham experience is something the locals don't have. Make the most of what you have; perhaps you need to re-visit your SP, Greg.'

'You sound as if you are an organiser of some sort?' asked Greg.

'I am. I'm an events manager at the SEC in Glasgow.'

'Wow, a big events organiser,' Greg stated.

'Yes well, just an event's organiser. Now here's the garage.'

A dark blue Nissan Ascona sat in the middle with ample room on either side. A work bench filled the back wall but there was something which Greg failed to identify overhead, above the car.'

'What's that up there?' he asked.

'When the car is out, of course, the table comes down and we fix these six wooden legs over here, she pointed to them strapped at the side. When it's set up, you have a full-sized snooker table.'

'Very neat. I presume you are not taking the snooker table with you?' asked Greg.

'If I want to play snooker, and that's quite doubtful, there are many snooker venues in Glasgow. I didn't play as much as my father and my brother. I don't want it.'

'Perhaps your brother might?' suggested Kate.

Sue's bottom lip trembled. 'Norman came off his motor bike three months ago. He did not survive.'

'I'm very sorry to hear that Sue. Our condolences,' said Kate touching Sue's arm lightly.

'You've had a very rough time,' said Greg.

'I know. I just want to sell and get away. Get back to Glasgow. This chapter of my life has ended.' Sue wiped her eyes with her spotted handkerchief.

'If you just wait a minute, I'll bring you something,' said Sue as she entered her home once more.

Kate and Greg looked at each other perplexed. Moments later Sue returned, dry-eyed.

'Here, have the agent's brochure. All the extra facts are in it, more than I managed to give you.'

Kate took the folder and placed it under her arm. 'We thought we might take a beach walk and give it some thought.'

'Excellent idea. Why not walk over to the King's Cave. It's not too far and the sun is trying to break through,' observed Sue.

'That sounds a good idea. The cave, Greg?' smiled Kate.

'Thanks for the brochure,' was all he said.

The sand was soft and golden. Kate took off her shoes and walked barefoot at the edge of the water. She looked back at the house. 'Not a better position on the whole island Greg. What about it?'

'What about what?'

'Come on, the house. Didn't you fall for it?'

'Not as much as you did, obviously.'

Kate stopped in her tracks. She looked out over the Kilbrannan sound and tears began to fall down her face. Only when the sobs were heard did Greg take any notice.

'So you've got your life fixed. Go ahead then, but leave me out.'

Kate's hands were on her hips. Her face, like an angry bull. 'Greg, what the hell are you saying? Do you want a divorce? Or do you want to talk things through? I've got the time if you have.'

'What's the point? I'm just ready to get home.'

Kate gave a large sigh and blew her cheeks out. 'Can you not just enjoy the time in a new environment. We've got four days left. Why throw in the towel today? Even if you can't get a gym up and working, what else can you do? Think about it. Think outside the box.'

'And don't you think I have? Don't you know I've been pulling my hair out, almost sobbing myself to sleep and coming up with nothing? Absolutely nothing and you know what's keeping me sane? Well, do you?'

Kate replied with a shake of her head.

'Well, I'll tell you. It's getting back to Fulham to get bodies fit and see some smiling faces. That's what is keeping me sane.'

They continued to walk. Kate replaced her shoes as the sand ran out and more taxing steps over boulders and hidden rock pools slowed their silent progress down. Kate wondered what Greg was really thinking. She could not accept he was only missing his work. He seemed reluctant to enjoy himself. Was he depressed? Her mind was active and the recurring thought was that he had found some new client at the gym and he was transfixed by her. She did not want to make a scene.

Soon the cave appeared and they approached its yawning mouth. Kate let out a howl and it echoed around the entrance. They walked deeper into the cave and she sat down despite the stones being wet. Greg was looking out to sea with his back towards his wife. When he turned round he saw Kate had removed her bra, was topless and was smiling at him. He hesitated. She began to unbutton her jeans.

'Christ, not here. This is a cold, wet, stony place if ever there was. Come on, don't be daft.'

Kate dressed smartly, disappointed she could not coax him towards her.

'Right, let's get back to the car,' she said.

6

Hardly a word was spoken as they continued up the west coast of the island. Despite the silence, Kate took note of the number of homes en route. She was by now convinced her mobile haircut service was viable, necessary, and desirable. The only stumbling block, and it seemed insurmountable, was her husband.

They were no sooner back at their B&B when Greg told Kate he was going for a walk. From the way he informed her, it was a walk he intended to take on his own.

'Not going out with Greg, then?' enquired Mrs. McSkimming.

Kate shook her head and raised her eyebrows. 'No, he wanted to go alone.'

'Men are often like that, they need space to think.'

'I think Greg had better walk to Lochranza and back. He's got a lot on his mind.'

Mrs. McSkimming smiled then uttered a short laugh. 'If he gets to the distillery at Lochranza, he might take a little longer. So, time for a cup of tea, my dear?'

'Oh yes, please. Just what I need, right now.'

Kate quietly stepped forward to see the bird feeder once more. She was still there when the teapot arrived.

'What a selection of birds you have. At home, we see starlings, blackbirds and a few blue tits, and of course pigeons. But that's about it.'

Mrs. McSkimming settled the tea service and joined Kate at the window. She patted away nothing obvious from her apron. 'The one on the left is a green finch, the ones pecking at the bottom are coal tits and blue tits; there's a grey wagtail and a stone chat on the edge of the lawn. You'll see the goldfinch in the morning. That's when he comes. He loves the seeds of sunflower hearts in the feeder.'

'Quite amazing, the selection of birds you have.'

'You should climb Goatfell before you go. A different species of birds you will find up there. Hawks, falcons, you might even see a golden eagle. They are about. Now tea, come and sit down.'

'Thank you. You are really thoughtful,' said Kate.

'So Greg has a lot on his mind? A holiday should unwind him, I'd have thought.'

Kate took the opportunity to offload her worries. She felt she could trust this homely host.

'I think I've found the right house, the right job, in a wonderful setting; the list goes on. But Greg? He tells me he's a city lad. He can't see his business as being transferable up here. One of us will have to stand down. And right now it's not going to be me.'

'I see. Well, perhaps the time is not right. Think about it again in a year or two, Arran won't disappear.'

Kate welcomed her suggestion. She needed some time to think it through so she changed the subject.

'Did you know Amal Zaidi?'

'The Zaidis? Did I know them? It was such a pity they left last year for good. You know, they had a trout farm? They employed a lot of staff up near Lochranza. What a delight they were. But you knew them?'

'Yes, Amal is one of my Chelsea clients.'

'Oh, of course, they live in central London, don't they?'

'Yes, they do.'

'Well, what a co-incidence, the Zaidis. The community was very sad to see them go. They supported many initiatives over the years. They loved it here. I think Amal's husband was much older. That was why they sold up and left. But the fish farm is still going strong. That's where I get my trout. Now have a ginger snap. I don't mind if you dunk it,' she laughed.

Kate took a deep breath. 'You know I can smell the flowers even from inside the house.'

'That will be the roses underneath the open window. They smell beautiful don't they?'

'There's such quietness about Arran. I'm sure it would be good for my blood pressure.'

'Remember you have come here in summer. We have good springs, usually some really warm days in summer and wonderful autumn colours. Winter is a bit of a downer but I've the Guild and a choir I sing in. Just a few of us but we enjoy it. Oh and not to mention the bridge sessions. That's the serious side of me,' Mrs. McSkimming said looking over the top of her glasses and sounding off a grunt perhaps indicating her loss of form at the square table.

Kate took her last sip of tea and replaced her cup onto its saucer. Her thoughts turned towards the evening. 'Where do you suggest eating tonight?'

'Let me see. Are you looking for a quiet tête a tête or a boisterous background to provide distraction?'

'My, stark choices. A bit of both perhaps? I've no idea how an angry bear eats in a restaurant.' They giggled like schoolgirls.

'Then I'd try the Crofters Music Bar for a distraction. Some fine traditional musicians play there. There are some snug tables too. Greg is bound to like that.'

'I hope so.'

'Mind you I have not eaten there myself but I've heard good results from their customers.'

'Tell me where is this place?'

'Och, they're on Shore road. I'll phone them up. Better book a table, they have only 40 places.'

The Crofters Music Bar was in full swing when they arrived. Their twosome table had been reserved and they had their backs to the sea. That meant they had a full view of a country singing set of four musicians. They sang in tune and harmony. They heard Country Roads first followed by Mary Black's Only A Woman's Heart. It was while they were singing Mary's song Kate drew close to Greg and whispered in his ear.

'Perhaps it's too soon to come to Arran. We can put it off for a couple of years.' She kept her eyes on him as he contemplated her words. But he didn't speak. He turned to her and kissed her cheek.

Kate was very pleased with her sacrifice. It put Greg in a happier mood. But in two years' time, would she still want to move to the island and would he kick up a fuss once more? She dismissed her thought. It was time to make amends.

They walked arm in arm that night along the sea front. Some yachts had lights on and lights twinkled on the mainland over the dark-lined horizon. They drew closer as fresh cool wind circled their steps. Kate informed him of the ornithological discussion she had had with Mrs. McSkimming and suggested a walk up Goatfell the next morning.

'A walk or a climb?' asked Greg

'A bit of both I think,' she replied.

7

On their last day, they climbed Goatfell. It was a gloriously hot and cloudless day. They had bottled water, fruit, and energy bars for their outing, but took their water sparingly. It was an arduous assault on the mountain for two Londoners. But they were not alone. Polite greetings were exchanged with early climbers on the descent. They saw groups of climbers above them and several behind. Looking over the Firth of Clyde, they saw a myriad of sea craft. They ranged in size from yachts to ferries and there were two submarines spotted as they sailed south above water.

'Greg, have you ever thought of having a boat? Or a small yacht with sails?'

'Where would we have it?'

Kate realised it was not practical and responded in fun. 'In the Serpent, perhaps?'

They laughed.

'I had a boat once,' said Greg.

'Really? You never told me about it.'

'It was painted red.'

'Honestly, I would have remembered if you had told me.'

'Well, I only had it for a couple of years.'

'Where did you sail it?'

'I grew out of it. It was a balsa wooden boat. I played with it in my bath.'

Kate guffawed realising she had been led into his story but she enjoyed the tale. It showed her husband in a more favourable light.

They reached the summit just after 1 pm and sat at the top along with a few other climbers. 'Great view,' said Greg to a couple nearby.

The response came in a Black Country Birmingham accent. 'Yes, we like it up here. Been thinking about coming up and settling in fact.'

'Really?' asked Kate showing great interest.

'Yeah. But my wife says we ain't got the money.'

'The lottery might come your way. Then you could come. What line of work would you have? I mean would it be the same as you have now?'

'Oh yes. No problem. I'm a chef. There are lots of positions in Lamlash and Brodick as well as hotels around the island. I'd find work.'

'What about your wife. Would she want to work?'

'Yes, I met her in the catering business. She's a waitress. We're a team. That's what we could offer,' he said.

'You need a team. You can't do it on your own,' added Kate.

'So you on holiday here?' the man asked unnecessarily, finding something to say.

'Yes, back to London tomorrow.'

'A long trip south. Stopping anywhere?'

'Yes, probably. Not yet decided. Depends on how far south we get, really.'

'The climb didn't hurt your plastered arm, did it?'

'No, as you see it's bound close to me. I got up fine. Hope the descent is the same,' commented Kate.

On their way down, time flew by. They felt exhilarated. They felt glowing and they felt very much in love once more.

It was with a heavy heart Kate sailed away from Brodick. She felt Greg was glad to be back on the mainland yet his body must have benefited from the island holiday. They realised they knew the island quite well having gone round it twice and climbed Goatfell. They had met many unrushed local people and found them welcoming. Kate hoped they would be back certainly before five years had elapsed, at the most. Then she might settle on Arran. However, that was not for discussion at present.

They returned to London two days later having stopped at Wigan on the way home. It was soon time to buckle down to the morning journeys to town which created their livelihood but the distance meant nothing to Kate's memories of Arran and the possibility of working there.

Greg seemed much happier as expected and to celebrate their return home, he brought three expensive bottles of New World Chile wine home on Friday. He was glad to meet up with his in-laws again.

'Well, island hoppers, how was it? Did you find your ideal home?' asked Lizzie before sipping her wine.

Kate passed around the bowl of nuts and looked at her sister's interested expression. 'We found the right house, didn't we Greg?'

'Snooker table, hot tub in the rear garden, jacuzzi in the bathroom, a bay window of miles of sea and distant land....'

'Distant land?' enquired Alan.

'Yes, Mull of Kintyre, as near as a stone's throw in places.'

'You know, Greg can exaggerate sometimes?' stated Kate and all of them laughed in agreement.

'So when will you settle there?' asked Lizzie.

'We've put it off at present. You know winter will soon be on our heels,' said Kate looking out of the window at their small garden in need of some TLC and hard work.

'Kate's right about that but we agreed to perhaps a two-year wait. When we're two years wiser,' said Greg with a grin.

'Even two years, less fit perhaps. No time like the present. Strike while the iron is hot, Greg,' said Alan.

'Yes why not?' asked Lizzie.

'All I can say is that there is no need to prepare a farewell party just yet,' said Kate.

Greg shook his head.

'Right, I think the lamb is ready. Let's sit down.'

8

It was closing time at Kate's Nuthatch hairstylists and she looked out of the window. The sun was shining and she felt good in herself. She would walk over to Fulham and walk home with Greg. But first, she had to change her duty high heels and wear flat-heeled sneakers. London pavements were hard and unforgiving.

She set off around 5.15 pm almost in a dream. She was coming to terms with the loss of the Arran house and the job. Yes, she may have two years to prepare in her mind. But the present meant earning well and preparing for what she thought was a common wish they had, to lead a less hectic life.

Not even Denmark Hill slowed her down. She too seemed to be a city girl and it was what she was used to. She continued to walk on the left side of the road. She passed several shops and flashed her eyes over the offerings behind the glass. A shoe shop saw her in navy blue court shoes and a florist seemed to offer some colour to her home but on greater inspection, she felt the blooms were already past their best. She approached the Love Walk Cafe at 81 Denmark Hill and casually looked in at the city workers delaying their return home for a half-hour over coffee.

She had just passed the cafe window but had to stop. She had seen something which seemed familiar. It initially horrified her. She had to have a closer inspection. She retraced her steps and looked in through the window. Greg had his back to the window and he was sitting with an attractive young woman. She thought for a moment. Was this a client, a secretary, a recent acquaintance?

She took a deep breath, promising herself not to jump to the wrong conclusion. She entered the cafe and made for the table.

'Oh excuse me, Greg, I was just passing. I thought we could walk home, together,' she said with charm, giving Greg an outlet.

Greg's mouth was open. He could not find the right words.

The young woman looked up at Kate. 'Walk home?' she queried.

'Yes, but I am not rushing you,' Kate smiled at her. 'I thought I'd walk home with my husband.'

The young lady's eyes enlarged and bore into Greg's face. 'You liar,' she screamed. 'You didn't tell me you were married. You're a scum bag. God, you are worthless and this woman, your wife, she must be daft having you as a husband,' she shouted as all the other tables focussed on the developing drama.

Greg could only hope the ground would open up and swallow him. How could he get out of his self-destructive moment?

The young woman took her coat from the coat stand which Greg had carefully positioned not twenty minutes before.

As she passed the table she left her best insult. 'The girls told me you were a philanderer. I was the fool who didn't believe them. Tomorrow they'll learn all about you, Don Juan. Oh god, I should have listened to them. What a fool I have been. Greg, I wish I'd never set eyes on you. They said you were a lecher with no spine. I didn't believe them. But I do now. Oh, and the promises of a new car; a holiday in South Africa and a weekend in Paris. Well, Greg, if I ever get these pleasures, they certainly won't be with you. I hope we never meet again,' she yelled. 'Anyway, you will end up in hell, and I'll not be there.' By now even the staff were motionless wondering if cups and saucers were about to fly.

They didn't. She made for the door. As she left she did not turn back but pulled the door closed, in anger. The door did not respond. It had a power restraint and closed gently behind her.

9

Kate was relieved that Greg did not come home that night. He had gone to stay with a male colleague at the gym, known to her to be gay. But the decisions had to be hers. Was he allowed one discretion? Was this normal for young men? Did not men have seven relationships in a lifetime, as one magazine informed its readers? Or was it the first, yet last straw? Could it let her break free? These thoughts multiplied in her mind, then died. They could only be answered by Greg and he had not made contact.

So it was a sad and unhappy Kate who went back to work the following day. Her colleagues tried to empathise with her, offering advice and the benefits of some, who were single women. There seemed to be many decisions to make, although Kate was not ready to make any of them.

She got through most of the week with the help of her hairstylists and on two occasions over a glass of wine after work. Friday dawned and the weekend loomed ready for a face down with Greg with all the cards laid on the table. The day dragged on. In the afternoon, she wondered if she'd take the time off, but Amal Zaidi had arrived and she liked Kate to do her hair.

It did not take long for Amal to see her distress and Kate felt able to share her recent sadness. Amal also sought her experience of her holiday on Arran. She heard of her mobile work possibility and the house of her dreams. But that had now crashed. She was unsure if she would leave their jointly owned house or if Greg would. Whatever she would decide would be a financial disaster. Amal saw she was a girl in much distress. She took Kate's arm. 'I'd like you to eat with us tonight. Can you?'

Kate could not grasp what she had been asked but there had been no expectation that Greg would be in touch with her on Friday, anyway. She needed time to be alone. But Amal was a great support to her and she knew Arran well. 'I'd be delighted to come tonight,' she replied. 'You are really asking me. I mean are you sure it will not be an inconvenience.'

'On Friday nights as Muslims, we pray at the Mosque then we eat. The men eat separately.'

'Oh, so it will just be the two of us?' confirmed Kate.

'And the cook, we eat with her too.'

'That sounds wonderful. What a very pleasant surprise.'

Amal took out her mobile phone and spoke Urdu for two minutes.

'My husband will collect you here at 5 pm.'

Kate wondered what else was said. Had Amal's husband agreed? It seemed she had her way and the lift would be appreciated.

Amal's haircut tip for Kate was larger than she had ever had from her before and she recognised it with a grateful bowing gesture.

Two hours later at precisely 5 pm, a Bentley car drew up outside the Nuthatch. A man entered wearing a smart peaked cap and enquired of Mrs. Kate Bailey.

Kate raised her hand and with a wave to the staff, she accompanied the driver to the car. The driver opened the back door of the vehicle where Mr. Zaidi sat. He beckoned her in.

'Good evening,' said Kate.

'Good evening. I hear you are dining with us. It is a great pleasure to have you.'

'The pleasure is mine I am sure,' she said politely.

'Not at all. You will be telling us of your adventure to my beloved Arran.'

'Oh, I thought I'd be eating with the womenfolk.'

'You are of course. But afterwards we make conversation.'

At 5:30 pm the car arrived at The Boltons in Kensington, known to Kate as the most expensive area in town. A servant opened the car door for her and she made her way up the stairs. A metal handrail supported Mr. Zaidi. 'I rely on such aids these days. My knees are quite weak.'

'I am sorry to hear that. There are so many supporting devices available.'

'Yes, and I have some in the bathrooms too,' he said laughing as the door opened and Amal stood before her. She was regaled in a very smart gold and red dress with a scarf lightly touching her hair and drooping down over her left shoulder. Kate felt much underdressed.

'Welcome, Kate.'

'This is most kind of you. What an amazing home you have.' Kate's head reeled around to take in the paintings, the quality curtains, and the period piece furniture before her.

'Allah has been very kind to us, my dear,' said Mr. Zaidi as he cleared the last step and entered his house.

'Come through this way, we are going to sit out on the lawn till we are called for dinner,' said Amal.

An old collie sheepdog struggled to get to its feet as Kate passed by.

Kate bent down to stroke it. 'You stay where you are my pet. No need to get up.'

'She won't easily. She's coping with old age, like us. We call her Corrie. You can imagine why.'

'After the Arran village, perhaps?' suggested Kate.

'Not just named after the village. That's where we got her.'

'Forgive me but I didn't think many Muslim families had pet dogs.'

'Yes, that's true but I can assure them Corrie has been the perfect dog and we've been lucky to have her for sixteen years.'

'Let's go over here and sit in the gazebo. We find deck chairs so low these days,' said Amal. The gazebo was a large wooden construction with ivy trailed around its base, secretly trying to climb before the pruners arrived. It held ten people comfortably but three sat down amid many coloured cushions.

'Orange or lemon?' asked Amal as she took a glass from the side table. Without asking she deposited an ice cube in it.

'Lemon please,' replied Kate.

Amal poured two lemon drinks and one orange squash for her husband.

'You know your husband's wish,' Kate said.

'He's allergic to lemon.'

'I see.' Then her eyes caught some motion. 'Oh look, the fish,' said Kate suddenly seeing a large golden Carp Koi rise to the surface in the nearby pond.

'Fish are very restful.....especially on a plate,' roared Mr. Zaidi with a broad smile.

'You surely don't eat these fish do you?' enquired Kate.

'No, no my dear. I unwind about now, in front of them as they glide around. They are my pets. Here watch this.' He stood up and from a small tub in the gazebo, he took out some fish fodder and approached the pond.

'Now look,' he said

The fish all responded to feeding time and Kate saw at least twelve fish fight for the best pieces of flaked food.

'It's hard to believe we are in central London. It is so peaceful here.'

'Yes, only the occasional stray flights seem to pass over head. It is very quiet. We've been here for fifteen years now.'

Kate's curiosity got the better of her. 'And may I ask what work did you have?'

He laughed holding on to his sizeable stomach. 'Wrong tense. Not, did I have. I am still working.'

'I'm sorry I did not realise that,' she replied instantly, almost in disbelief.

Mr. Mohammad Zaidi sat back and looked towards the sky. 'I took over my father's business when he died and built up my empire, in oil. I've been trading oil ever since. But now in my eightieth year, I manage my portfolios. Money makes money you know. It's where you put it, that's the skill.'

'And he's very good at that, I might add,' nodded Amal.

A call from the house summoned the women to eat. They made their way to the kitchen while Mr. Zaidi filled up his orange juice again and sauntered around his beautifully laid-out garden.

The women sat down on a carpet cross-legged. They were served with a plate of lamb stew and several hot chapattis. Amal showed Kate how to tear off a piece of bread and gather the stew. Then in one swoop, it was raised to the mouth. Eventually, Kate gave up and used the spoon which had been provided for her to accommodate this traditionally eaten meal.

'So you were on the cusp of living on Arran, it seems.'

'Yes, I was set on it but Greg wasn't. Now I know he had other things on his mind. I should have guessed as our love life had disappeared too.'

'Then divorce is on the cards?'

'I can hardly believe what I am saying but I see no other way out.'

The plates were taken away by a servant and a rice pudding arrived with a scoop of chocolate ice cream balanced at a precarious angle on top. This time they both had spoons and both had a sweet tooth.'

They joined Mr. Zaidi in the spacious lounge for coffee served with after-dinner wafer-thin mints.

'You have been very kind to me. It came so unexpectedly too. Just at the right time,' Kate smiled.

'The right time? I thought you were at a cross road,' suggested Mr. Zaidi. 'Tell me, Kate, if you close your eyes what do you see?'

Kate leant back and closed her eyes. She did not have to think long. 'I'd be at the house we saw, I'd be in my mobile hair dressing van and I'd be home at night to watch ships go by through the telescope and I'd be as happy as I could be, with Greg left in London to sort out his life.'

Mr. Zaidi smiled. 'I am eighty-one in two months' time. As you know we loved Arran so much. We sold our property there and it would give me great pleasure to make your dream come true.'

Kate opened her eyes and sat up straight trying to understand what was being said.

'This house at Blackwaterfoot. You liked it?'

Kate suddenly had dreamy eyes. 'Yes, we were planning to sell Greg's business and the house and start up in this beautiful home.'

'Who is selling the house?'

'Err, Rightmove, it is.'

Mr. Zaidi opened his laptop and entered Rightmove, Arran. Then he entered Blackwaterfoot. He approached Kate. 'This is the property isn't it?'

'Yes, that was my dream house,' she said clasping her hands and holding her breath for a moment. She felt an excited calmness wash over her face.

'And it's still on the market at £235,000K.'

'Yes. They are selling as one parent has died and the other has dementia and is in a care home. She wants to sell to pay for her mother's care.'

'Admirable. Then I don't want to reduce her asking price.'

'But what are you doing?'

'What am I doing? I'm buying the house for you, of course.'

'But you shouldn't. I'm not your family. You should care for them first and not spend money on me.'

He looked up at his wife and then his eyes fixed on Kate's. 'We had two sons and a daughter. The oldest son died last year and his widow is well taken care of in Cairo. My daughter is also in London and her husband takes good care of her. Our youngest son is in the family business and he will get a share of this house when we've gone. So, I've attended to all my financial affairs. Now let me continue.'

Kate looked at Amal. Her eyes were those of a satisfied woman proud to see some of her husband's wealth being given to a worthy cause.

'This hairdressing van. Leave that with me. But you can't socialise around the island without a car. I'll contact Broadway Auto Care Car Sales tomorrow. You went to Arran with a Ford Kuga. How was that?'

'It was a good car.'

'Then a Ford Kuga?'

'This bill is mounting,' Kate said grasping her skirt over her knees.

'But it comes with one condition. I'll come to that.'

'The telescope is part of the price?' he asked looking at the house details online.

'Yes, that was agreed,' Kate replied, glad that an additional cost could be avoided.

'Is there anything else, darling?'

'Perhaps a starter kit to get things moving.'

Kate screwed up her eyes a little bit. 'A starter kit?'

'Yes, a bit of cash should come in handy, to stock up provisions at the start. Of course, you'll have to organise the divorce, transfer your bank account to Arran, get house insurance, car insurance updated, notify friends, etc. You will be busy, I'm sure about that.'

'I'm lost for words, I really am.'

'I'm not. We're going to put this plan into action as soon as possible. I'm going to run you home. You use tonight to get all the things you need. Those you could pack into a Kuga and the rest to be forwarded through a removal agency. I'll sort that too.'

'I think I am dreaming. Is this really coming true?'

'Yes, it is and so let's get cracking. Let me run you home. Tomorrow will be your last day at Nuthatch.'

Kate hesitated. 'You said there was one condition?'

'Ah yes. I had nearly forgotten. When you are settled and next year sometime in summer perhaps, expect two visitors. Am I making myself clear?'

Kate stood up and approached Amal. She hugged her. 'Of course, you can come, at any time. After all, it's your house on Arran.'

'No it's not, it's your home,' said Mr. Zaidi opening his arms wide to receive Kate. She clasped on to him but felt a kiss might not be culturally acceptable. Then he kissed her.

10

Kate clipped her shears to her heart's content in a dream the following day, having let her colleagues know that it would be her last day with them. Naturally, they learned about her plans to move away but they also had to swear not to inform Greg where she would be, should he enter the shop.

Shortly before closing time Mr. Zaidi parked outside Nuthatch and waited for Kate to finish work. She entered his car after hugs from her saddened hairstylist colleagues, whose tears were on show for all to see.

'The sale of the house went through effortlessly. Your car is being given its final check and a full tank. A firm in Glasgow will provide a made-to-order hairdresser's mobile vehicle and Chariots of Chelsea will complete the house clearance. They will be at your home at 6 pm this evening.'

'Then I'd better get a move on.'

'Then let me take you to collect your Kuga.'

Kate felt on top of the world. She squeezed the steering wheel as she left the garage. Was this really happening? Twenty-four hours had never been so traumatic. She would be forever indebted to the Zaidi family.

The Chariots of Chelsea van had blocked off two drive entrances with a driver at the wheel to prevent angry words from returning resident drivers.

Kate took command to identify her needs without taking too much away. The removal men were understanding and careful. They informed her that her goods would be taken into storage for two days before they would be able to go to Arran.

Greg would remain in the house she decided. Vindictiveness was never her trademark. She texted him to inform him that she was leaving. The house would be his. But she never told him of her good fortune or where she was about to go. She told him to return to the house in two days' time. Finally, she informed him that the period of separation was part of the divorce proceedings now underway.

Greg's response was contrite and instant. He was grateful he could return to the house although unsure how she was able to leave without financial security. He accepted divorce was the right course and wished her well.

Kate took to the road early the next day and got as far as Carlisle. She booked into the Crown and Mitre hotel for the night and from there, booked her sailing to Brodick for 2 pm the next day.

The crossing was so rough that Kate filled a convenience bag like so many other passengers on that sailing. Gone was her plan to have a late lunch on board. She sat down, took off her shoes, and lay flat across a long varnished wooden bench. She felt both miserable and yet fortunate, as an hour was the scheduled length of the sailing, and that was a mere moment of her new life. After twenty minutes she sat up and shortly afterwards a female passenger sat beside her.

'A really rough crossing today,' said Kate needing some conversation after a lengthy drive.

'Yes, just our luck. I reckon I sail back and forth ten times before I catch a storm. Mind you if it's a serious storm, the boat does not sail. I think the decision must have been touch-and-go today,' she said sorting her handbag. 'On holiday?' she asked.

Kate was tempted to say 'yes' but for the first time, she could confidently state her new situation. 'No, I'm on my way to my new house at Blackwaterfoot.'

'Ahh, a new resident. That's what I like to hear.'

'It will be a significant change for me. You can possibly guess I'm from London.'

The woman sat forward to inspect Kate. 'Aye, London to Blackwaterfoot? You must be a first. What a contrast. I hope you settle.'

'I think it easier to settle this way than from Blackwaterfoot to London.'

'I'm not so sure. Many of our youngsters leave the local school, attend further education and rarely come back to work on the island. Many travel south.'

Kate nodded in agreement after reflection. But the conversation was interrupted.

The intercom requested drivers to attend their cars. Kate made her way unsteadily downstairs to the lower deck. She held the rails to find her car. There was a deafening sound of car horns activated by the ship's movement but soon she spotted the Kuga and was glad the voyage was coming to an end. She sat in the car watching others fight their way past cars, like drunken sailors, towards their own vehicles. She waited and waited. A further announcement informed her that landing was difficult. The ship would stand off Brodick until it could safely dock at the harbour.

One and a half hours later, the ship docked securely and Kate drove four hundred yards to the Brodick Co-op. There she spent almost £95 on food, provisions, cleaning essentials, and fruit. Then as the rain hid most of the island, Kate crossed the B880 road to Blackwaterfoot. She drove carefully making sure the misty rain did not hide potholes. She felt close to the Golden Eagle in the height of the String road. But it was a lonely road with almost no traffic on it.

She heard a buzz from her handbag. A text had arrived. She looked into her rear mirror. The road was not straight. She dared not stop to receive the message. She continued on her way looking for a lay-by while wondering who could be calling, the Zaidis, the Chariots of Chelsea Removals, Rightmove, Greg? The thought passed her mind whether to change her phone number but for the time being, there might have to be some communication even with Greg.

Seven minutes later she entered her new hometown of Blackwaterfoot. She crossed over the bridge on the twisty road in the village centre and proceeded slowly towards her new home. Once more a text buzzed in her handbag. She parked in the drive and opened it. She had indeed two messages.

The first text was from Rightmove informing her that the front and back door keys were under the coconut mat at the front door. The second text was from Greg. She held her breath as she opened it. She read it twice to make sure she fully understood what he was saying. But the message brought a smile to her face. The Crown Prosecution case was bringing no charges against the lorry driver or the Baileys following the M 6 accident. That was good news.

She turned off her mobile, placed it in her handbag, and got out of the car. She managed to carry a large heavy case inside and then walked around her new home. She entered each room with a smile. On the kitchen table was a vase of flowers, a tray of fresh bread, biscuits, milk, and cheese was in the fridge. The note was from Sue. She wished her a long and happy life in the house. Kate went to the kitchen cupboard. Inside were two canisters. One marked coffee the other marked tea. She took them out and gave them a shake. She smiled. Then put the kettle on.

Even before her large case was removed from the hall, the front door bell rang. A shudder went through her body. Christ, not Greg was her initial thought. But then realised he could not be there. She walked through to the front of the house not recognising a lady standing waiting for the door to open.

'Good afternoon. Welcome to your new home. I hope you will be very happy here. My name is Madge Orr. I'm your new next-door neighbour. I couldn't help being nosey. May I suggest as you have just arrived, that I invite you for a meal this evening?'

'Oh my goodness. How kind you are,' Kate said stepping forward to shake her hand. 'I'm Kate Bailey'

'And bring your stookie too,' she laughed pointing to her plaster.

Kate had learned a new Scottish word. She was sure to remember this one.

'And bring your husband too, of course,' Mrs. Orr added.

'Err...I'm single. No husband to talk of.'

'What, a young good looking girl like you? There's many a young farmer's son who will want to meet you,' she said smiling from ear to ear.

'That might be too much a challenge for a city girl.'

'Enough,' Mrs. Orr said. 'Then 7:30 pm suit you?'

'Yes, that would be fine thank you. Your gesture is very much appreciated.'

At the appointed hour and after a hot shower, Kate arrived at Mrs. Orr's next-door house. She was a woman in her early seventies and had a picture of a man on her lounge wall. Kate just had to enquire.

'My that's a handsome photograph,' she said looking at it.

'Aye, that's Donald, my late husband. He had a trawler fleet. He's been gone just over three years now.'

'I am sorry to hear that.'

'Thank you. But I have two sons who took over the fleet and so you'll meet them when they drop in. Now come away through. The soup is on the table.'

Kate looked at the thick broth and the pearls of barley floating at the top. It was just what she needed after a long journey from Carlisle.

'Now, do tell me what brought you to Blackwaterfoot.'

'I fell in love with the place and wanted to get away from London. Unfortunately, my husband didn't want to move. So we had our arguments and I'm here and he's in London, pending a divorce.'

'Oh, I see. I am sorry to hear that.'

'Don't you worry about that, Mrs. Orr. He will not visit Arran again.'

'Oh I'm Madge; call me Madge, no need to use my Sunday name.' She passed the ground pepper to Kate.

'Now, Kate, will you be working, or are you a young lady of leisure?'

Kate sighed then focussed on her hostess. 'I was a hair stylist in Chelsea. I thought my skills would be transferable, so I'm going to have a mobile haircutting service up and down the west side of Arran.'

'No, you are not my dear, are you? Get away wi' ye.'

'Well, that's my plan. Don't you think it will take off?'

'Take off? My dear girl, you are a godsend.'

'I'm so glad to hear that.'

'And you'll not have to advertise. When I tell a few people it will spread like a burn in spate. But you'll have to get rid of that plaster.'

'I'll make an appointment at the Brodick hospital tomorrow.'

'Just turn up ma dear, tell them you are resident on Arran and show your plaster.'

Early the next morning Kate set off to the Brodick War Memorial hospital. She drove up the incline and parked on the left. It was a warm Redstone building; not at all like the London hospitals. It was quiet. No blaring ambulances were around.

She reported to reception and the matter was quickly diagnosed. It meant a breaking of the plaster, an x-ray to see how far the bone breakage had mended, and either a new plaster or no white stookie again.

That is how it turned out. No new plaster. Kate returned to her car. She held both her arms out. The injured one was paler than the other arm and many more dark hairs were on it too. She rubbed them. Many came off straight away. She decided a shower when she got home was what she needed.

11

Her call to the Arran Banner in Brodick seemed excessive in Mrs. Orr's eyes but she felt it would do no harm. She made the call.

'Good morning. My name is Kate Bailey. I have started a new business. Can I speak to a journalist?'

'Hold the line, please. I'll see if one is free.'

Kate held the line wondering if a menial hairdresser's launch would have enough interest for the island's paper.

'Hello, Mrs. Bailey? Hugh Boag here, editor, how can I help you?' he asked in a professional manner.

'Call me Kate. Well, I am about to start a mobile hairdressing van on the west side of the island.'

'Sounds a great idea to me, Kate. Have you much experience as a hairdresser?' asked Hugh.

'That's something I've never really been called. I was a hairstylist in Chelsea for the past eight years.'

Kate could hear a pen scratch the editor's notepad.

'That begs the question, why come to Arran, especially the less populated side?'

'The hectic pace of life and lack of meaningful human contact made a change feasible. Yes, the quieter side of Arran but with a mobile van, I'll cover some ground, meet the people there and yet enjoy the solitude. My recent divorce was the tipping point and this significant enterprise finally became a reality through an Arran lover.'

'And who might that be?' asked an interested Hugh.

'The Zaidi family. You possibly knew them.'

Hugh took an audible deep breath. This woman seemed to have significant contacts.

'You know the Zaidis?' asked Hugh.

'Yes, a client of mine who had a fish farm near Lochranza. They came to it every summer for around twenty years, I think.'

'That's right. They owned the fish farm. I think they left a couple of years ago.'

'Yes, they did but their hearts are still on Arran. They will holiday here in summer, at my home in Blackwaterfoot.'

'Okay, I've a story here. Let me take your mobile number. And can you send a photo of yourself?'

Later that day she heard a rumbling noise. It came from the front of the house. Then it stopped. She went through to the lounge. She saw what had caused the commotion and waved.

As she went out to welcome The Chariots of Chelsea, she stopped and a shudder ran through her entire body. Her heart missed a beat. Her thought was clear. The first item off the trailer was not hers.

'Hi boys, this isn't mine,' she said with brows gathered in confusion and disappointment.

'Oh yes, they are. Mrs. Zaidi visited yesterday morning before we left and put these lady's golf clubs and bag in the van. She put a note inside.' The older removal man, George, put his hand down the bag and produced the note. He looked at it and tried to flatten the fold he had created when extracting the letter.

Kate took it from him. 'You boys ready for some tea?'

'Sure am,' said one, and the other said 'Milk and two sugars for both us – identical.'

Kate boiled the kettle then took the kitchen knife to slice open the letter.

Amal informed her that she had been on the ladies golf committee at Lochranza but the course at Blackwaterfoot was an ideal course to start on. The course had only 12 holes, spectacular views, and a residents starting fee of £160 :

'It is an ideal way to meet friends and promote your business. It's on your doorstep. But it's not called the Blackwaterfoot Golf Course! It's known as the Shiskine Golf and Tennis Club. Enjoy your days on the course.'

'Tea is ready boys. Come through to the kitchen.'

'Thank you, Mrs. Bailey.'

The two men arrived, pulled out chairs from the table, and sat down beside plates of pancakes and fruit scones.

'Wow, this just ain't London town, is it,' said the younger man, Paul.

The men laughed.

'By the way, was there a tennis racquet as well?'

'No, I don't think that was mentioned, was it, George?'

'No, but golf takes time. I wish I played golf. Too expensive at home and too busy,' said Paul.

'A tiring and uneventful journey up north?' asked Kate.

'It was okay,' said George. 'We've been as far north as Shetland one time. You get to see the country that way. First time on Arran though.'

'George says it was okay. I think he forgot we just missed killing a deer on the motorway. That gave us a fright.'

Instantly Kate replied. 'Where was that?'

'Where was that Paul? Was it in Lancashire?'

'No, it was passed there, somewhere in Cumbria,' replied Paul through a mouthful of scone.

That evening at a leisurely pace, Kate found a home for her furniture. Then from her numerous bags, she filled drawers and cupboards. The house had become a home and at 10 pm that night, with a cup of Ovaltine gripped in two hands, sitting in her lounge, she looked out over the sea and saw the twinkling of lights. Campbeltown was still awake as were the fewer lights shining at

Carradale. She smiled to herself at the fortune she had secured in the most beautiful part of a stunning island. Her arm was free of its plaster and she had come to terms with the whiplash injury. Nothing could possibly go wrong here. If it did, she pondered, she had clubs that could serve as a deterrent, and they'd also help to heal the occasional whiplash twinges.

12

The following morning was a depressively wet day. It was not the fine mist that she had encountered before but driving rain made the coastline of Kintyre completely disappear.

She lifted her mobile and contacted Amal.

'Hello, Kate here. Thank you so much for the golf clubs and bag. I have walked past the golf club before and admired its condition, but if truth be told, I've never played golf.'

'Maybe not, my dear, but if any friend visits, who plays golf, then a set is ready for them. But do give it a go, Kate. I was not very good at first but I enjoyed the fresh air, and you have marvellous views over your course.'

'I'll give it some thought. And guess what? I'm out of my plaster.'

Marvellous. There's no stopping you now. I'm so glad about that, my dear. Now I can tell you a firm in Glasgow designed and finished your haircutting van. I am sure you will like it. It should be arriving today or tomorrow. Then you will be up and running.'

'I don't know how to thank you. This is really quite remarkable. Speaking to you has cheered me on a very wet day.'

'Wet where you are? Then it's all over the country. We are wet in London. And I know where I'd rather be.'

On that damp thought, the conversation ended amid laughter.

Kate did venture out to The Harbour Shop and apart from some routine purchases, she bought a copy of the Arran Banner.

Back home she sat down at the kitchen table and opened the paper. On page 18 she found the picture she had sent together with her intended work and her telephone number. She wondered if Madge Orr would have read the Banner.

The following day was much brighter with a fresh breeze blowing inland from the sea. Yet it remained very quiet where she lived.

The hairdressing van arrived that afternoon. After the drivers had left in a car that had followed the van, Kate went in to inspect her new workplace, her environment where she would renew her cutting skills.

The van had a pleasing light crimson colour exterior, with a white roof. There was one cutting chair and a bench for either the customer's children or the next customer. Above were cupboards under lock and key. When opened, there were as many hair ointments and lotions as you could imagine. Under the desk were three electricity points for dryers and a hot water tank that fuelled the hair washing procedure. A further cupboard held towels, capes, and tissues. Enclosed at the back was a small but important loo. Kate was ready to receive her first customer.

That turned out to be Mrs. Orr next door when she dropped round to see Kate with a bag of freshly harvested Victoria plums.

'I should be cutting your hair inside. It seems odd to cut it in the van in the drive.'

'But this is where you will have all those Chelsea preparations. I'm looking for a new look entirely?

'A radical or slight change?' asked Kate.

'As radical as you can make it without looking absurd,' she said looking over her glasses frame. 'But I don't want to be a Punk or have a Barnett!'

Madge left satisfied with a cropped style at the back of her neck and a bob of white hair neatly falling over one side. As Kate was cutting, her telephone messages were accumulating.

She opened her diary along with a national grid map of Arran. Once she had identified where the customers were, she was able to group them into Pirnmill, Achencar, Machrie, Blackwaterfoot and Kilmory communities. She phoned them all to tell them when and where their appointments would be.

Pirnmill was her most northern point and she had four ladies requesting an assortment of hair-dos. Her appointments began at 10 am and after lunch, she had two remaining heads to attend to. During the sessions, Kate had to reveal much of her past before receiving nuggets of information and gossip about the locals. But her first day was going well.

At 4 pm, she said goodbye to her last customer of the day. Then she did her accounts. They did not take long, of course. As she tidied the van, she saw a man approach with a hurried step. Was this her first male customer? He politely knocked on the side of the van.

'Do you wish a haircut,' asked Kate to this unkempt red-headed and red-bearded man. He nodded as Kate opened the door. He came in and saw the chair. He made for it and sat down.

'Cut it on top and cut my beard. Do you do beards?'

'Yes, I'm trained to do all sorts of hair treatments, although I admit I've not cut a man's hair recently. Not for a long time have I had such a challenge. But I'll make you a new man.'

'A new man? Yeah, just what I want,' he said.

'That's a Welsh accent you have not so?' asked Kate as she placed an apron over his front.

'Good with accents are you?'

'Not really, just strong national ones I think. So Welsh?'

'I've not been in Wales for some time.'

'Difficult to lose accents. My English accent is unlikely to become Scottish overnight,' she said enjoying the banter of the moment.

He chose not to speak after that initial dialogue for some time. But Kate had a pressing question. 'You are not a natural redhead. You have had a henna treatment. What do you want me to do? Keep it red or let it return to its natural colour?'

He seemed to understand but took some time to decide and reply. 'Can you make me blond? A number 2 over the head and my beard off.'

His instructions were clear. He seemed to want to become a new man indeed. Kate was not sure of him. He was not even like the most difficult customer she had dealt with in Chelsea. Yet she could not put a finger on his attitude. Her questions dried up as the shears stripped his head of its matted locks.

Her sharp-bladed scissors cut down his beard before she lathered his face in preparation for a close shave. She held his chin as the blade made its cleansing mark on his face. His eyes seemed to be enlarged, fully alert, and angry. It may have been a domestic situation he had come from. She would not pry any further into this enigmatic individual. When she finished, she took a warm damp cloth over his face and returned the flannel to the basin. But she did not have to remove the apron. He had already done so and was standing up staring at Kate.

He pulled a small knife from his pocket. Kate saw it. She gasped.

'Where's the money?'

Kate was not going to be foolish and went to the drawer she had recently locked. She opened it and lifted the notes. As she did so, she saw her mobile phone. She closed the drawer smartly. She stretched out her hand. 'Take it and go,' she said in a firm and almost threatening voice.

'Come here.'

'Put that knife away first,' she demanded in a shaking voice.

He hesitated. Then he collapsed the blade and returned the knife to his pocket.

'Come here.'

The man was tall, rough, and ready-looking. What his instruction meant she dreaded. It was very threatening. She froze to the spot.

He approached. He grabbed her around her arms making her arms immobile and forced a kiss on her lips. She turned her head away. He kissed her neck. Then he grabbed her blouse and ripped it apart. Now she was convinced he was going to rape her. However, she remembered what Greg had once said if she ever found herself in this predicament. But she had to be in the right position. She thought of a ploy, hoping it would free her.

She relaxed. She no longer fought to set herself free. 'I've a condom packet over there.' She pointed vaguely to the rear window. 'Let's use that.'

He was unnerved. Her co-operation was not his experience but her suggestion was music to his ears. He donned a smile at her as he released her. He turned to watch her as he set her free to fetch the condoms. She opened a drawer by the back door and found a small powder bag, she knew she had there. She raised it. 'Here they are. This is where I keep them.'

He undid his fly and brought out his penis in preparation. As he took his hand away to stretch for the condoms, Kate took one step nearer him and launched her foot with venom at his testicles. He groaned in pain and fell to the ground.

Kate did not hesitate, she left the van and ran onto the main road as fast as she could, hoping to stop the first car she encountered. Having run hard for almost two minutes, she slowed down and looked back. She saw her attacker stagger out of the van. She feared he would follow her so she continued her run. She ran and she ran without sight of a car going in either direction. Another full three minutes elapsed and a further look behind, but the road had curved and her van was no longer visible. It was then she saw a car appear. She stood in the road with her hands waving giving an impression of someone warning cows might be on the road but when the driver saw her torn blouse and terrified look, he dove to the side of the road and stopped. He got out of his car.

'Are you alright?'

'Have you a phone?' Kate asked shaking as she did so.

'Yes, here, take it.'

Kate took his phone but her fingers shook so much she could not identify the three numbers she had to use. 'Please, can you dial 999?'

The man, still trying to assess what the trauma had been to her, took the phone and dialled. The Lamlash police officer, Sergeant Rory Murdoch, was at Kilpatrick. He spoke to Kate, who informed him of her recent attack. He asked where the van was. She told him. He said he would be there in fifteen minutes and she was asked to stay with the man who dialled. She was more than happy to do so.

The man was the local minister, whose clerical collar was hidden by a silk scarf but Rev Colin Craig knew where his duty lay. He asked Kate to enter his car and wait for the police. Kate saw a bible in the back seat and what looked like a sermon case. She felt safe in his vehicle.

Eventually, the police car with flashing blue lights appeared and drew up behind the minister's car.

Rory Murdoch, the experienced sergeant, got out of his police vehicle.

'Mr. Craig. Just as well you were in the vicinity.'

'Yes, a tragic event. Just not what you expect on Arran.'

Kate got out of the car.

'I see your blouse is torn. You've been through the wars?'

'Yes, I'm sure he was going to rape me.'

'Okay, Mr. Craig, you will be a witness, for your part only. I'll call at the manse tomorrow and get the details from your angle. I think I must concentrate on the assailant. So 10.30 am. How does that suit you?'

'I've a funeral in the morning. Jessie White.'

'Jessie White from Imachar Point? She was a good age.'

'Aye, ninety-seven. So anytime that suits you in the afternoon?' suggested the minister.

'Okay, I'll ring you before I arrive,' Sergeant Murdoch said turning over another page of his notebook.

'Now Miss, what's your name?'

'Kate Bailey.'

'Was that you in the Banner? Starting a new hairdressing service on this side of the island?'

'Starting? It was my first day.'

'Oh, dear. Well, let's hope it will be the worst day of your life. Let's get back to where it all started.'

Kate was told the van would be part of the investigation and he would run her home at the end of the day. They returned to the van. They entered and Kate gave an exact reconstruction of events. Sergeant Murdoch was pleased to note the red-headed and bearded assailant was now a blond with a clean-shaven face. That he had a Welsh accent too. These were very credible statements and super evidence.

'My god we are in luck here,' he said. He pointed to the floor. 'Red hair. Is that his hair?'

'Well he arrived with a henna colouring and he left a blond.'

'But that is his hair?' he asked again while setting his eyes on Kate.

'Yes it is,' she replied unaware of the significance.

'Then we have good Welsh DNA.'

13

Sergeant Rory Murdoch brought Kate back to her house and as the police needed to hold on to her van, the sergeant asked that she took time to recover in the knowledge the Criminal Injuries Board would financially compensate her for her injuries and time off.

Kate took comfort in knowing her assailant was not local but he was at large on the island and the Banner announcement had mentioned she lived in Blackwaterfoot. She did not sleep easily that night.

She informed her neighbour Marge of the events of the first day and she agreed to lock her doors and windows at night too. 'You know I've never done this before.'

'What, you never lock your doors?' asked Kate.

'No, no need. Usually.'

Kate smiled for the first time that day. 'Of course, Arran is not London.'

Kate was still recovering from the shock of the day the following morning. She needed to get out of the house. But go where? The answer lay propped up in the corner of the hall.

She put on her bottle green jersey and dark brown slacks with tennis-type white shoes. She placed her waterproof jacket in the golf bag and set off to the Shiskine clubhouse two hundred yards along the road.

She entered the clubhouse where a man was opening a new box of balls. He looked up at her and did not recognise her. She was out of her comfort zone and he soon knew it.

'Can I help you? I'm Mike, the professional here.'

'My name is Kate and you see I have a bag of clubs. But I've never played in my life. I want to give it a try.'

'Well, you have made a good start. You have come to the right place. We have a 12 hole course here and it's a great place to start. The holidaymakers usually play 18 holes so they don't come here as often. We welcome beginners of all ages.'

'That's encouraging. So do I just set off from the first hole now?'

'No, you set off from the First Tee. But wait a moment.'

Mike opened the clubhouse door and shouted. 'Bruce, can you spare a moment?'

'Coming,' he replied.

Bruce entered the clubhouse and Mike introduced him to Kate.

'Bruce, can you take Kate around the course this morning?'

Bruce eyed the young lady with interest. 'I'd be delighted,' he said.

'Do I pay beforehand or after?' asked Kate.

'On your very first trial round, there will be no charge,' the professional confirmed.

'Really?'

'Yes, but if you are resident, and you return, it will cost you £160 for a year's subscription.'

'Well let's see if you are a natural, shall we,' said Bruce offering to open the door.

Before standing on the first tee, Kate was taught how to address the ball. She thought she'd start with some humour to relax Bruce. 'I know how to address the ball,' she said. 'Good morning ball,' she bowed to it and then looked to see Bruce laugh with her.

That got them off to a jovial start and Kate was pleased to recognise the big-headed driver before she was introduced to the club.

Bruce got her to swing the club and then he stood behind her. He was much taller and lean. He placed his arms over her shoulders and held the club asking her to hold his hands as the swing took effect. Then he showed her how his body swung through the stroke and she tried to do it keeping her left leg secured to the ground and her right leg ending up on tiptoe. Bruce told her she was ready to start and they made their way to the first tee.

Kate insisted that he play first and so he asked her to watch what he was doing. His ball flew off straight down the fairway and a long way. Kate knew she did not have his strength and told him so, although it was an unnecessary truism.

She took up her golfing position, placed her ball on a wooden tee, stood back, and took some swings to release any tension she had in her body then went through the routine recently learnt. First address the ball.

She secured her footing, concentrated on the white sphere, and then she swung back the club. Swoosh. The club cut through the air without hitting the ball.

'I guess golf is not for me, Bruce.'

'Nonsense, everyone misses a few times before they are comfortable with the clubs. Have another go. Keep your head down. Don't lean back.'

Kate took her time and then released her swing. She heard the ball click this time and saw it fly down the centre of the short grass.

'That's the way. Straight and a good distance. Not bad, not bad at all. You should be proud of that shot.'

'Beginners luck, you really mean.'

During the round, Bruce and Kate got to know each other better. He had been aware of the Arran Banner article, knew she was a hairstylist, and learned of her tragic first day. He felt sorry for her. Devious Mike had perhaps asked that he take her round her first golf course, as a blind date, but he dare not suggest that to Kate.

She learned that he was a novelist who also provided an editing service and contributed to a monthly page to a writer's magazine. He had not always written. He had served in the Navy for fifteen years before retiring, three years ago. It was not long before each knew they were contemporaries.

At the end of the game, they sat in the clubhouse drinking coffee.

'Well, I think you did very well in your first game.'

'That's kind of you to say so. I had some wayward drives with the iron clubs.'

'We all do at times. But your approach work around the greens was particularly good.'

'Not the complete game though.'

'If you chip one shot and putt in the hole the next; that's two shots. Only two. So if it takes you three shots to reach the green, and two to down the ball in the hole, you will make a very good golfer indeed.'

'I hear what you say. But I think I'll need a few more rounds to get better.'

'Then perhaps you would let me take you around again?'

'Yes, when could that be?' she asked and on reflection, somewhat in haste.

'10 am in two day's time?'

'But don't you work during the day?' she quizzed him.

'I usually work in the afternoon and the evening. I get most of my writing done in the evening.'

'I see, then on Wednesday, that is if it's not raining.'

'Whether it is raining or not, I'll be out. Golf does not respect the weather. It is just another challenge.'

That night Kate opened her computer and typed in Bruce L Butler and found his website. She saw he had been nominated three times for the Booker Man Prize and two of his books had been taken on by the ARTE film company. She went onto Amazon and bought one of his books which she would read at her leisure and with pleasure.

14

Sergeant Murdoch telephoned her two days later as she was munching her Cornflakes. He seemed hurried.

'Hello, Kate. Some interesting news. Perhaps I should say developing news. My colleagues in Wales have identified a suspect who has not been seen for over a year. They have sent a picture of Mullard Davies. He seems to be the guy you identified. I need you to see it. Send me your e-mail and I'll send the photo to you. Get back to me as soon as you can, whether you recognise him or not. This man is wanted in connection with the murders of two young children in South Wales. He has a knack for changing his name and his appearance and we are getting more police from the Ayrshire mainland to track him down.'

'That's a great relief. Mind you he is still on the loose isn't he?' she asked combing her fingers through her hair.

'Loose yes, for the time being. I'll keep you informed.'

Thanks that's a great help.'

Before Kate could open her e-mail, Hugh Boag from the Arran Banner called her mobile.

'Hello Kate, Hugh here from the Banner. We're going to run a 'Wanted' front-page spread on Mullard Davies. The police will be sending posters around the communities all over the island. We are working with them to get this man in custody as soon as possible.'

'But I've just been talking to Sergeant Murdoch. He wants me to identify Davies,' she said with a confused frown.

'Don't worry, that's a legal requirement. There's no doubt it's Mullard Davies we need behind bars.'

'Will you be mentioning my name and what happened to me?'

'No, that is sub judice at present but we will print "that following an incident near Pirnmill when a woman was attacked, the police were called to the scene. The woman was found injured and in shock." We'll keep your name out of it at this stage.'

'Well, let's hope they catch him.'

'You have no idea how useful you were.'

How do you mean?' asked Kate listening hard to follow the events being revealed.

'Well, you changed his henna hair to blond, got rid of his beard, and given him a close shave on his head. We have an excellent description of him now and I believe the hair is a good DNA sample of this Welshman.'

'But won't that identify me as the mobile hairstylist?' she asked in a confused and worried tone.

'Don't worry your work won't be in print. It's what I know about your case. I'll only print that after his conviction.'

After her second call, she opened the Sergeant's message. She downloaded the attachment and found her assailant staring at her with penetrating eyes. She returned the message.

'That's him 100% no doubt. It was him who attempted to rape me.'

Her van was promised back to her in three days. It needed that time to identify all traces of activity in the van. As it had been spanking new, there were fewer doubtful marks and any semen found would have come from the only man ever to have been in the mobile hairdresser's workspace.

The sound of Bruce's telephone call competed with Kate's Guatemalan coffee beans being reduced to fine grains, that morning.

'Hello, Kate. I hope it's convenient to talk?'

'Yes, of course. I had just made a coffee,' she said wracking her brain to wonder why the call.

'Fully recovered from the round of golf?' he enquired.

Ah, that's it. Arranging another round on the greens, she thought. 'So when's the next round? I'll have to be a resident member from now on. Must get my money's worth,' she said somewhat nervously.

'Actually, I was not thinking about golf. I wonder if you were free to join me for an evening meal at the Kinloch Hotel.'

Kate froze. Yes, she liked him. She had even bought *The Parrot's Tale*, one of his books. But she had hardly been on the island a week, not quite two weeks from her marital bed, and thus his offer seemed like an introduction to something she was not entirely prepared for, although she had no objection to his suggestion.

'Are you still there?' he asked.

'Yes, ...ye.. err...I'd be....delighted. Thank you,' she stammered.

'Then perhaps we could meet in the foyer at 7:15 pm? How does that suit you?'

'7:15 pm is just fine. It's not too formal is it?' she found herself say just in case it was a function he was attending and in need of a partner.

'Smart and casual, I think that's the term.'

Smart and casual seemed to sum up Bruce, she thought. 'I look forward to that very much.'

Sergeant Murdoch was having a planning meeting with a Skype to the Welsh police when the secretary insisted he took a telephone call. He went through to the office to take it.

'Good morning Sergeant Murdoch here.'

'Hello, Jim Ross here, from Lochranza. My motorbike has been stolen.'

'Mr Ross, a stolen motorbike? Well, all I can do right now is take its number and inform the ferry. I'm afraid it's not a priority just now.'

'But it's a motor bike and I'm in Lochranza. SN17ALN. Nobody steals up here. But I saw him leave. That's the thing about it. I did not know who he was. He had blond hair.'

Rory had a copper's instinct on hearing this. 'Did he have a beard?'

'No, no beard. He was clean-shaven.'

'Was he of a good solid build?'

'Yes, that would describe him,'

'Was he comfortable on the bike, I mean did he know how to ride it?'

'He certainly did. He freewheeled it from the drive then jumped on to start it, and off he went, over 45 mph still in the village.'

'Which way did he go?'

'He left by the Youth hostel, definitely heading south on the east coast.'

'Thanks, Jim. I've noted that. I hope we'll get your bike back soon.'

Sergeant Murdoch returned to the conference room with a smile. 'Okay Swansea, you still there?'

'Boyo, we certainly are.'

'Did Mullard Davies ever ride a motorbike?'

'Come to think of it, yes, that was his mode of transport down here but I remind you that was a year ago. I thought by now he might have graduated to at least a Mini.'

Motor theft on Arran is like snow on the equator. A motorbike has been stolen not far from where Davies was last sighted. One and one make two in my book, thought Murdoch. That's one for the lads. I had better inform them. That's what Rory Murdoch did and shortly afterward he learned that the Police Helicopter spotter had been alerted and would sweep the east coast that afternoon.

Kate heard the faint propellers in the distant air as she relaxed with a cup of tea in her back garden that afternoon. She wondered if that had something to do with Mullard Davies' capture, for only a brief moment. She had decided to erase as much of the incident from her mind. Anyway, her thoughts were concentrating on her meal with Bruce in a few hours.

15

In a knee-length dress of blue satin and a white cardigan over it, Kate set off to the mere 550 yards to the Kinloch hotel. She arrived at 7: 20 pm to find Bruce spruced up in brown flannels, a cream open-necked shirt, and a speckled brown and crimson jacket.

They entered the dining room and as Kate looked round the spacious tables, she saw four strange pictures on the rear wall. She let out a gasp of astonishment.

'These are copies of Alessandro Gallo's work. The animal heads with the human dress are both comical and at the same time profound.'

'You know your art,' she said as a compliment.

'When I'm in London, I sometimes visit the art galleries. I learn a lot about the artists' work that way.'

'So how often are you in London?'

'Usually three or four times a year,' he replied without giving any reason. Kate was not going to let him off the hook. London was a place she knew well.

'Is that work or just pleasure?'

'Bit of both really. I only see my literary agent on one day; the rest I head for museums and restaurants, before returning home to Arran.'

'I see. I don't know much about an author's work,' Kate said lifting the menu.

'I could have had an agent in New Zealand. I'd not have to go there but my agent Mandy Steel Collins and I like to meet every so often to see which publisher is interested in my latest book. We talk about book festivals and arranging author appearances and visits too. It's good to have that personal touch, in such a lonely profession.'

Kate gently nodded as Bruce spoke. His world seemed so far from hers. She returned to more practical matters. 'Have you seen the menu?'

'You go ahead. It's already committed to my memory.'

'Then you come here regularly?'

'That would be sad. Table for one, please. I've been in Blackwaterfoot for the past three years. They change the menu of course but I know their standard menu.'

A waitress approached almost with a skip. 'Can I get you some drinks first?

'Are you a wine drinker?' Bruce asked.

'Yes, I'll have a Merlot, please,' replied Kate.

'Is that a large glass or a small one?' asked the waitress.

'Er...I think a small one.'

'And you sir,' she asked with a tantalising smile.

'You can always have another small one later Kate,' Bruce said having noticed her hesitation. 'I'll have the Usige Dubh.'

Kate looked at him with a puzzled stare.

'Black Water. It's a dark beer.'

You speak Gaelic?' she asked realising he was not speaking English.

'Èisd ri gaoth nam beann gus an traogh na h-uisgeachan. It translates as 'Listen to the wind upon the hill till the waters abate'. What it means is – 'Keep a low profile until trouble passes'.'

Kate smiled at his erudite knowledge. The interpretation was so apt in her life.

'I've lost much of what I once learned in school. I remember many Gaelic proverbs though. They come in handy, especially in London.'

This revelation intrigued Kate. However, her mind was elsewhere as her eyes moved around the menu.

'I suggest the Arran lamb. That is of course if you are not a vegetarian?'

'No, then it's the lamb. I really like lamb. Is that what you are having too?'

'No, I'll have a plate of the Kilbranan seafood.'

'Ah the marmite of the sea,' she said, which surprised him.

'Londoners love their cockles and mussels. Billingsgate is such a busy fish trading place and there are so many good fish mongers around. But, the shellfish? Euch! Some enjoy it while it makes so many others sick. I'm afraid I'm one of those.'

'So far you have learned I speak Gaelic and you are neither teetotal nor vegetarian.'

'Surely we have something in common?' asked Kate only too aware that they came from different backgrounds.

'Golf?' he said without hesitation.

'Golf, of course.'

They laughed quietly so as not to disturb the other diners but Kate felt everyone knew Bruce and she, a mere hairstylist, was creating her publicity, in a different league.

The night sped by and when it was time to leave, Bruce knew she was separated from her husband and Kate knew he was a bachelor, having found no mate aboard ship then drifting into the solitude of writing.

They agreed to enjoy another game of golf after Kate had enquired if their time together was hampering his creative work. He told her his inspiration came from meeting new people and she should not be surprised if she appeared in his next book. She inquired about the story. He told her it had no reflection on her but *The Crazy Psychologis*t was its working title.

Understandably Kate asked to be escorted back to her house by virtue of Mullard Davies'sunknown whereabouts and there, on the front doorstep, they casually embraced and a first brief kiss was shared.

On waking the following day, a familiar noise was heard at the front of the garden. Her van had arrived back having spent the last three days in police custody.

She was pleased to see her workshop once more and went out to inspect the tarnished van. However, when she opened the van door, her nose was met with an invisible cloud of air freshener. She entered and everything seemed to have been polished. The van was looking immaculate inside and out. The police had returned this scene of crime into its former glory and she was keen to put that memory behind her and set off to cut hair once more. But first, she made a note to place her telephone in a drawer near the exit.

The telephone rang at Lamlash Police station as Rory Murdoch sorted through his mail.

'Hello. My name is Anne Baxter. I live at High Corrie. I opened the curtains this morning and there is a motorbike in the rough area behind my back garden. It's on its side. No one seems to be around, I think it is abandoned. I thought you should know.'

'Yes indeed. Never hesitate to call the police if you think something looks suspicious. Right, I'll send an officer to see it. Don't go near it. Don't touch it. We may have to do some work on it. In fact, there might be a few officers interested in this. Thank you for informing me. Thank you very much.'

'So I did the right thing?' Anne enquired.

'Yes, you did. But stay locked in your house. It will soon be very busy where you are,' said Rory realising what could be about to take place. He then telephoned his colleagues to inform them of this development and, on the mainland, they realised the helicopter had a more specific area to cover.

Kate set off to Corriecravie, no more than a hamlet, but one in need of haircuts. She seemed to have the whole community queuing up. Blue rinses and darkened brown hair dyeing were the order for the day and trimming and cutting most heads. Kate's second day was much more relaxing but what irked was that everyone wanted to talk about her ordeal. They had made the connection having read The Banner's article about the new service and the woman assaulted, by word of mouth. They had the story confirmed as they sat having their hair requirements attended to. What pleased Kate was their desire to fill her diary in a further six weeks' time and this venue was not far from home.

Before returning to her house, Kate locked the van, crossed the main road, and ventured towards the rocky shore. She was prepared. She had a plastic bag in her pocket. She reached the water's edge and began to collect as many different types of seaweed. Soon her bag was filled with Bladder Wrack, Marsh Samphire, Sea Lettuce, and Kelp. She returned to her home and immediately laid out her seaweed on the kitchen table. She then laid newspaper over her flat boiler and on top of it she separated each type to dry.

The helicopter, with three police officers on board, two of who were armed and the other with a taser at the ready, flew over Arran's northern coastline and followed the contours of Glen Sannox.

Mullard Davies was not deaf. He correctly thought the helicopter was after him. He found cover in the rocky Saddle facing Cir Mhor. Such was the denseness of the cover; it was not likely that the helicopter would easily find him. All he had to do was wait till darkness fell. The wooded copse 200 yards away would be an obvious spot to investigate and through the rock crevices, he could see if they came that way.

The helicopter hovered over Fionn Choire, unable to land on the gradient, and three officers descended by cable. The helicopter then flew off to nearby flat ground at Loch Tanna, still in communication with the officers.

The ground was hard and foliage thick. There could be many hiding places. The police officers decided to call off their search for the time being and request tracker dogs to be brought to the area.

Kate had all her seaweed dried and brought out the Bladder Wrack. She pounded it to tealeaf-consistency. Then she made a cold infusion. All that was left was to mix it with rhassoul clay. She placed an order with Amazon.

16

Bruce called round in his golf attire on Saturday morning as Kate gave her hair concoction another mix. She had completely forgotten that she was to be playing golf that morning.

'Oh, Bruce. I'm sorry. Make yourself a cup of coffee while I get ready, will you?'

He smiled. 'No rush, there's no starting time on the first tee.'

Kate opened her wardrobe in a panic. What should she wear? Her fingers ran along the rail. She chose a red turtle-necked jumper and the smartest, if tightest, pair of trousers. She took two steps at a time down the stairs.

'That's me ready. Finished your coffee?'

'Not quite. Tell me, are you a scientist? I mean this looks like a chemist's workbench,' he said pointing to the seaweed mixture.

'That's awaiting Rhassoul clay.'

'You have lost me there. Is this a cottage industry you have up and running?'

'I never thought of it that way but Arran's seaweed is on my doorstep. My clients need the nutrients to thicken their hair. Especially my older clients whose hair can be so thin.'

Bruce said nothing but he looked through the window into the distance. He then turned to face Kate.

'I think I can help you,' he said in a ponderous manner.

'I doubt that very much, Bruce. Hairstylists and authors seem a world apart to me,' she rattled back at him then laughed.

They were on the 6th hole with Kate on par with the putting but still having trouble staying on the straight and narrow of the fairway.

'We are in for at least a week of this fine weather,' said Bruce.

'Then perhaps a break from golf. We could go for a swim tomorrow afternoon,' she suggested.

'Picnic lunch?'

'Sounds good to me. What time?'

'What about I drop round at midday and we set off from there?'

'Yup, I'm happy with that.'

'By then, I might have some good news.'

Two Alsatians, Rock and Roll, had served faithfully in Police Scotland, as active canine detectives for five years. They were in peak condition and their handler Sergeant Dave Dawson lived with both dogs. They were transported by helicopter to Loch Tanna then they set off in a north-north east direction with the scent of Mullard Davies' henna hair, in their nostrils.

The dogs were in their element. They were trained not to bark until the culprit was detained, frightened, and submissive. All of a sudden both dogs turned back 180 degrees. They ran along the mountain face until Loch Nuis. There they stopped to drink the cool fresh loch water. The dogs tracking devices secured to their backs led the pursuing officers along the banks of the Garbh Allt stream to the Standing Stone at Monyquil. Passing the Chambered Cairn, the officers followed the B880 until they had to cross the Macharry Water getting their No 2s wet in the process. Meanwhile, the dogs had slowed to an almost walking pace. That was either a good sign or a sign of dejection.

With the summit of An Tunna above them, they passed the old fort and turned right up Gleann Easbuig. The dogs were only one hundred and fifty yards in front.

Then both dogs stopped and barked loudly. The officers picked up the pace. Mullard Davies tried to run away but the two dogs had him covered. As soon as one step was taken to the right, Rock would pounce forward making Mullard go the other way to face the growling jaws of Roll.

The officers now saw the terrified criminal and knew that his time on the run had come to an end. They telephoned for motor assistance to be at Glenloig car park as soon as possible to take Mullard into police custody.

Mullard Davies stood with his hands high shouting at the top of his voice to take the dogs away from him. The instruction was given and as soon as the dogs turned, Mullard set off towards the summit. A taser was aimed and Davies fell like a puppet's final pose.

He was grounded and handcuffs secured around his back. Thereafter the twelve-minute trudge back to the police car got underway and Arran could sigh with relief, Mullard Davies was captured.

17

Sunday morning was just as Bruce had said. A bright blue sky with a hint of a wayward cloud seemed of little importance. She prepared a picnic with sandwiches of cheese and ham; two pieces of cake she had made the previous night and washed a pear and an apple. She added two Tunnock caramel wafers for good measure. She filled a bottle of cold water and then got out her swimwear. She rejected her bikini. That was too revealing for what was really only a second date so an aquamarine one-piece was what she wore and she put her shorts and a tee-shirt over it.

Bruce drove up and parked in her drive. He opened the rear door of his car and brought out a hamper, a windbreak, and his picnic.

They set off on the short walk to the shore and Kate took off her sandals to walk in the sand once more. But the sand was hot, so she walked nearer the water where the sand was wet but firm. That was when her phone rang.

'Oh I'm sorry, I should not have taken it with me. I'll switch it off after this call.'

Bruce shook his head as if to say, this is the modern businesswoman. But that was not the topic.

'Sergeant Murdoch. Yes....wonderful news. That really has put my mind at ease. Thanks. Bye.'

'Look, that's it switched off,' said Kate as she returned the phone into her beach bag.

'Sounded like good news.'

'Good news? Mullard Davies has been caught. Isn't that great?'

'Yup. So a trial in Ayr. Then Swansea awaits,' said Bruce.

'I thought his two child murders were still outstanding. If they are, then a murder takes precedence surely. Two murders in fact. That will mean a life sentence; my case is in the minor league, as it were.'

'I hadn't thought of that. I suppose you are right.'

They continued to walk hand in hand further along the deserted beach. 'Let's stop here. Any further and the ground is tricky.'

'Okay, here?'

Bruce speared the windshield down into the sand and rolled out a rug. He spread it over the flat area he made with his foot. They sat down and opened their picnics. They shared their sandwiches. Bruce preferred Kate's as she had added some chutney to her cheese.

After they completed their lunch, Bruce lay back in the sand and Kate did too a moment later. Their hands touched and Bruce held hers as he broke his news.

'You remember I told you I was in the Navy?'

'Yes. Fifteen years you said.'

'That's right. Well, I am still in touch with another officer, Mike Weeks. I telephoned him last night. We spoke for about half an hour before he put me on to his wife Carole.'

'Goodness knows where this story is leading.'

'It will soon be clear, Kate. Carole works for Boots. She is a buyer. You know someone on the lookout for new products to take them to the store. Well, I told her about the natural resource here on the Arran coast and what you are doing with your hair products. She also saw a seaweed market for soups, vitamins, toothpaste, shampoo, and meals. They do exist, of course, but Arran has a selling point, she said. She'd like to meet you.'

'Meet me? Here on Arran?'

'Well, either Arran or London.'

'Oh, that gives me a dilemma.'

'A dilemma?' asked Bruce.

'Yes, I'd love to see London again, but not Greg. The Zaidis I'd visit and the staff at Nuthatch but I'd also like to show her Arran. Gosh, I can't make my mind up.'

'The Zaidis? There was a well-liked family around Lochranza with that name. He employed many to work at the fish farm. Nice couple.'

'You know them well, Bruce?'

'Oh yes, my father used to go shooting with him.'

'That's them. I owe them a lot. Let me tell you how I know them.'

It took a further half-hour to explain all the details to Bruce, even if she had told him some of the facts before. Kate felt she had revealed all about her good fortune, possibly even prematurely. Nevertheless, they were both ready to take to the water.

The water was, of course, cold at first but within moments they were both swimming in the Kilbrannan Sound. They frolicked like school children in the waves. Two dolphins popped their heads up nearby. Kate called to them and they seemed to come closer, giving the impression they understood her command. They did understand humans played in the water, and so did they.

Mullard Davies remained handcuffed after being formally charged with the attempted rape of Kate Bailey, the theft of money in the hairstylist's van, the possession of an offensive weapon, and the theft of a motorbike. Then secure in the custody Serco Prison van, he was driven to Swansea to stand trial for the murders of Lin Owens and Abigail Jones.

Two days later, Bruce telephoned Kate.

'Hi, darling. I have to go to London. My agent wishes me to call. Would you like to come with me?'

Kate was excited. 'When would that be?'

'Next week Monday?'

'Yes, I could do some things down there. How long would we be there?'

'Three days. Can you fit that in?'

Kate hesitated as she contemplated a moment's crisis in her mind. 'Where would we stay?'

'The Corinthia. I always go there. Quite near the literary agency too.'

'And how will we get there. It's a long drive,' she stated thinking of all the arrangements required.

'Yes, it's a long drive but a short drive to Glasgow Airport and we're there in an hour and a half.'

'Of course, silly me. That sounds wonderful. Yes, a bit of me misses London.'

When the call ended, Kate hesitated. Bruce hadn't mentioned two single rooms being booked. However, she had other things to occupy her mind.

Kate lifted her phone and with her heart beating she dialled.

'Greg? Kate here. Let's be adults about this. We both want to go our own ways.'

'Yes, music to my ears.'

'I'm going to go for divorce by reason of adultery,' she said.

'Bit harsh. You've no evidence,' he replied.

Kate's heart missed a beat. 'I don't want to make this messy. You heard what that girl told you, about all the others who warned her? Remember? Or were you wondering how I would have reacted? Then if not adultery, certainly unreasonable behaviour.'

'What does that entail?

'You as the respondent formed an improper relationship with another person during our marriage; as my spouse, you were unwilling to engage in sexual relationships with me; lack of emotional support given and your unwillingness to talk about the problems within our marriage. Pick any one from that list.'

'I see you have been doing your research. Found a new man I suppose.'

'I have not spoken about your current relationship so there's no need for me to talk about any of my friendships.'

'Where are you?'

'In London,' she lied so as not to entice him north but it was also a convenient lie. She told him she would be seeing David Tagg, her solicitor in Fulham next Tuesday at 3 pm. If he wished to be there, then she'd welcome that.

The flight down to London was uneventful. But Kate's heart was in her mouth. Had he booked separate rooms or would it be one room with a double bed? Would Greg be reasonable or vindictive?

The taxi brought them to the Corinthia by mid-day and Bruce booked into his usual room at reception.

'Kate, if you wish, you can share my room?'

'An extra room would be too expensive. I think I'll share it with you. That is if you are agreeable?' she smiled coyly.

He smiled back at her and then collected her bag and they headed for the lift. The room was large and square. Great long blue and golden curtains draped down the window. Kate separated them to see the view. Her London. Her city of birth. But no longer her home.

'I've got to see Mandy this afternoon, so I'm going for a shower, okay?' said Bruce.

'Yes, I'll come in after. I'd like to freshen up.'

Bruce ran the shower then stripped off and entered without locking the door. Kate noticed that. She undressed and waited sitting on the bed with a towel wrapped around her. Bruce seemed to take ages. Then she heard the water turned off.

Kate entered the bathroom as Bruce dried himself. She put her towel on the chair and entered the shower. Soap bubbles fell over her shoulders and in a rush, she washed her body. When she opened the shower door Bruce had gone back to the bedroom. She dried herself in the bathroom, then wrapped her towel around herself and entered the bedroom to see Bruce combing his hair in the nude.

She approached him and rubbed his back gently. He turned around and undid her towel dropping it to the floor.

'There is always a first time in a relationship. And we're in your home town. How appropriate,' he said running his hands over her hair.

He lifted Kate and gently laid her on the bed. Their lips met. They kissed and then their kisses slipped down their bodies. Within a few moments, the act was initiated and Kate felt two powerful emotions. One that she had found a new life partner and also, that if Greg had known, he could perhaps divorce her, for adultery.

18

Kate's visit on Monday afternoon was to The Boltons in Kensington. She arrived at their gate and approached the intercom. She pressed the button and a voice inquired who the caller was.

'I'm Kate from Arran,' she said into the mesh square. Immediately the gates began to open and through the enlarging gap, she saw Amal running towards her.

'My dear, it is so good to see you again. A visit or...'

'Only a three days' visit.'

'Then do come in and tell me all about Arran.'

Over a china cup of Assam tea served in the gazebo, Amal learned of the rocky start to Kate's Arran business.

'But they did catch him?'

'Oh yes, by now he'll be in custody in Swansea, and on two murder charges, he'll be an old man when he gets out and unlikely to visit Arran again, the scene of his Scottish crimes.'

'It's really is so good to see you again. I've missed you,' said Amal tapping her knee.

'And I must thank you for one other thing. The golf clubs.'

'Ah yes, have you started to take up the sport?'

Kate looked coy all of a sudden. 'I'm getting instruction.'

'And is that from the professional at the club? He's very good at that.'

Kate cast a playful eye at Amal. 'No, a member. He's been showing me how to play, and in all honesty, if I can stay out of the rough off the fairway, and give a good putting service, it keeps my scores down, he tells me.'

'That sounds promising.'

'I think you know who he is.'

'Really?' asked Amal with a cocked head.

'Does the name Bruce Butler ring a bell?' she asked expecting some recognition of his name.

'Does he ring a bell,' she said emphasising each word. 'If only he remembered ours,' she laughed. 'When he was a boy he would climb our tree and pinch an apple or a pear. He loved his fruit. He thought he wasn't seen but I saw him. Boys will be boys. I didn't have the heart to stop him.' She sipped her tea. 'And Mohammad went shooting with his father. Ah, such memories. ...so you know Bruce?'

'Yes, we've been playing a few rounds over the course.'

'I heard he left the Navy. He had served his time, as it were.'

'Yes, and now he's an author?'

'Indeed, an author, like his father.'

'I didn't know his father was an author,' said Kate with a look of surprise.

'Well, he only wrote one book. But that makes him an author doesn't it?'

'I suppose so,' said Kate feeling out of her depth in the discussion.

'It was not a novel, more a textbook. I remember it was about the diplomatic service in the Middle East. That was his last posting.'

'What was his work?'

'Diplomatic. He had been an Ambassador. Egypt was his last post and of course, that was of great interest to us. They were a delightful family. Sadly Bruce's father died a year after retirement. Not uncommon for some to find retirement hard to adjust to. His mother, some say, died of a broken heart. The doctor's certificate was more accurate; she died of a heart attack. Bruce, being the only son, took over the family home at South Feorline near Blackwaterfoot. But perhaps you knew that?'

'Yes, I must be totally honest with you. I'm here in London to renew some contacts but also to initiate divorce proceedings. I took the opportunity to come down with Bruce who has a literary agent's meeting with his agent Mandy Steel Collins. We are staying at the Corinthia hotel.'

'And Kate, darling, would I be right in thinking it's a meeting of two lost souls?'

Kate looked sheepishly down at her feet and then lifted her eyes. 'I had no intention of starting a relationship so soon after leaving Greg, but love is a mysterious force. We were drawn to each other over golf and it is something neither of us can resist. So it was your golf clubs which brought us together,' she laughed.

'You have found more use of them already than I ever have,' and their laughter brought her husband into the garden.

'What's all this chatter and happiness? I'm missing something,' he said approaching Kate and shaking her hand.

'Just girls' talk darling. I'll tell you later.'

On Monday night, Kate and Bruce dined at the hotel. There was a reservation on Kate's part and one which Bruce noticed. He could not put a finger on it.

'So how did your meeting with your agent go?' she asked.

Bruce gave a wide grin. 'Got a publisher for it. They are also interested in a film contract too. That'll all be done by e-mail back home. And you, how were the Zaidi family?'

'You like fruit?'

'Err yes, but we've not had the first course,' he said confused with a screwed-up forehead.

'You've always liked fruit?'

'Where is this leading? I see a wicked smile on your face.'

'Do you buy fruit from the shop or do you climb trees for apples and pears?'

'Oh, I see. Going back into my youth.'

A wide smile came over Kate's face. He understood she had been delving into his past.

'What else did Amal tell you?'

'Sadly your parents have died and that you have inherited their home at Blackwaterfoot.'

'True.'

'And...that your father was a diplomat.'

'I can't deny that. But you are still looking ill at ease. What's the matter, Kate?'

Kate opened her mouth and closed it twice. The words were not coming easily to her mind or lips. Eventually, she said: 'Six weeks ago I thought I was reasonably happily married. I arrive in Arran in an emotional state, faced a major trauma, and suddenly meet you and I've fallen in love. It's the Pygmalion saga all over again. Plain girl meets handsome Prince, who shows her how good life could be,' a tear fell from her face.

Bruce brought out his folded white handkerchief and offered it to Kate. She took it and dried her eyes.

'Look at it from my perspective. My youthful years passed by in the Navy. I decide to take over the family home, near Blackwaterfoot. I'm in need of friendship, companionship. I put it out of my mind. I was beginning to think it would never happen. My situation I'd obviously shared with Bill, the golf professional, and of course, it was him who got us together.'

'All that is true, I understand. But our backgrounds are not similar, in fact, they are poles apart,' she revealed her concern from the depths of her heart.

'No, I know that. But does it matter? I've found a very attractive, successful woman and one I want to share the rest of my life with, and that's a fact.'

'Successful?' she uttered. 'A separated London hairdresser, now with a mobile shop, on a Scottish island. You call that successful?'

'Darling, you really know your trade. You are a hairstylist, not a barber. On Wednesday, before we fly home, we will have a meeting with the Boots buyer. That's a real success. That's very creative. That will stand you out from the crowd.'

'Are you ready to order, sir?' asked the waiter.

'Can you give us a few more minutes?' replied Bruce.

'Certainly sir,' he replied.

That night, Kate felt Bruce had stated his case well. This was a permanent relationship for them both. In bed, she turned and cuddled him. Somehow in the morning when they woke, they were in the same position.

On Tuesday, Bruce was going to the British Museum while in the morning Kate was heading to Nuthatch. Then, in the afternoon the most important solicitors' meeting would take place. She would need Bruce's shoulder to cry on that night.

She arrived just after 11 am at Nuthatch to a warm cheerful reception. They were anxious to hear how the mobile hairstylist was progressing and she sat down to tell them three times, as each hairdresser came back from their client. She chose not to tell them about her ordeal but talked about her golf on a beautiful course and she did not mention Bruce either. She did ask if Greg had visited and was told twice. On each occasion, he enquired where she was but her secret was safely retained by the staff.

After a lonely lunch at a sandwich bar, she set off at 2: 30 pm to be in time for her appointment with David Tagg, the solicitor.

When she entered his office, Greg was already seated in a chair in the waiting room. She sat down three chairs away from him on the same line so that their eyes would not meet.

'I hope you are well,' said Greg.

'I am, as I hope you are too.'

'I was worried about where you were living.'

The sentences were short and specific. How many would be lies thought Kate?

'You don't have to worry about me,' she said.

'Still in London?' he inquired.

'I'm not giving you my address.'

'I know you left Nuthatch.'

Kate remained silent and Greg stopped his interrogation.

It was a relief when they were called into Mr. Tagg's office.

He shook both parties' hands. 'Hi, call me David.

Now let's start off with what I know. You Kate are the Petitioner seeking divorce on the grounds of adultery.'

Greg shook his head. David waved his hand at him. 'As you can imagine, adultery is extremely difficult to prove unless it's a position agreed. Mr. Bailey, I gather you protest against the ground of adultery?'

'Certainly, there's no evidence,' he stated and Kate threw her eyes to the ceiling.

'Okay, first I have to clarify some details. I presume you both live in England or Wales. You have been married for over one year and you are both in agreement to have a divorce, agreed?' David did not look up to see the response. There was no reply. He was fumbling through some papers. 'I have your address Greg, I can't find yours, Kate.'

A bolt ran through Kate's body. She waited for further instruction.

'No, I don't seem to have it.'

'Err, I don't want my former husband to know my address,' she said.

'Of course not. Perhaps you can write it down on this sheet,' he said offering her both pen and pad.

She wrote The Corinthia Hotel and handed the sheet back to him.

He read her note. 'Permanent address?'

'May I have the paper back?' she asked as a thought came to mind. This time she wrote c/o Zaidai, The Boltons, Kensington.

David looked up at her. His eyes fixed on hers and they smiled. He knew exactly where that was. He told Kate it was necessary to have her address for communication. So we need at least one to be resident in England or Wales or the case has no validity in the court.'

Kate sighed quietly. She made a note to contact Amal as soon as the meeting was over.

Greg could not understand why she seemed to have two addresses. Was she flitting between two of her hairdressers' homes? That was his only conclusion. She seemed to be on hard times. Those reasons made him want to get the divorce over as soon as possible.

'Let's see if we can agree on the reasons for divorce. Unreasonable behaviour? Now, who will start? What about you Greg?'

'I don't deny I have been aloof and withheld mutual sexual contact with my wife. I was also caught by her in the company of a woman I was dating.'

'More of a girl than a woman, I would have thought,' said Kate recalling the encounter.

Mr. Tagg raised his hand to order them to desist from counter-accusations.

'She was younger, I agree.'

'So you agree to dating another woman, unfaithful to your wife and withholding sexual gratification?' asked David.

Greg nodded.

'And Kate, you do not disagree about what Greg has said?'

'No, I don't.'

'Well, that makes my job easier. I can lodge these papers tomorrow. Now, I must ask you both to sign at the bottom of the page. In a nutshell Divorce on the grounds of Unreasonable Behaviour by virtue of infidelity. That will be sufficient to achieve our joint purpose.'

'And what is the timescale of the process,' asked Greg.

'It's hard to say. Depends on how busy the divorce courts are. Three weeks to set a date; about three more weeks to hear the case. I can represent you both, in this case.'

'And must we be in attendance,' asked a concerned Kate.

'No, not if the case remains unopposed. You don't have to attend although many do. They see it as the legal end to an unhappy time.'

The meeting was over and it was a relief to them both. They stood up then shook David's hand. As they left his room Kate enquired if she could use their toilet.

'Of course,' said David, used to this ploy to get away from an ex-husband. As he showed her the way, Greg gave his parting shot.

'Kate, I wish you good fortune.'

She turned round to have a last glimpse of her husband of seven years. 'Thank you. I wish you well too.' Then she visited the bathroom.

When she came out, she asked to see David again, briefly. When he came out of his room she handed him a sheet of paper torn from her diary.

'This is where you should address any future correspondence to me. Please tear up c/o The Boltons and the Corinthia hotel.'

'Ah, Arran. Lucky you. I did not really think you were living at The Boltons. And presumably you are down for a few days staying at the Corinthia. I've taken note. I regard your address as confidential.'

'Yes, that's good.'

Greg was pleased how the divorce proceedings had gone and brought out his diary to note six weeks hence.

19

Breakfast was a rushed affair. They had lingered too long in the bedroom that morning. But they were not late to meet Carole Weeks at her Boots office at 50 Newington Green.

'So delighted to meet you two. You must come and stay with us some time. Mike would love to see you again, Bruce, and to meet Kate.'

'Yes, that would be good. Or a holiday up at Blackwaterfoot?' suggested Bruce.

'Two options I'll have to put that to Mike.'

'Okay, time for me to leave you two ladies to chat. I'll be back in an hour. That okay with you Carole?'

'Sure, an hour should be fine.'

Kate gave Bruce a nod, unsure of how the meeting might develop. Bruce made his exit. Kate felt exposed.

'When these two boys get together, they natter like old women. We younger girls have our own agenda. So, a hairstylist entrepreneur. Just what we need, someone with practical hair solutions.'

'It's all a surprise. Bruce saw what I was doing making a hair paste out of seaweeds. It's not new. It's been done before.'

'If I sent you to buy a car, which make would you chose?'

Kate understood her point.

'Yup, they are not always the same. I want to find a selling point within the Boots range, for hair products; edible seaweed in pastes, and seaweed in pill supplements. Toothpaste too. You are following me?'

'Yes, Bruce gave me an insight into what he thought you could do.'

Her eyebrows jumped up. 'Really? Probably info from Mike, and he doesn't really know my role.'

'Your selling point,' questioned Kate. 'What about Seaweed in My Hair?'

'Seaweed in My Hair,' Carole repeated, contemplating the words as her eyes were fixed on the ceiling. 'You know, I think you've hit the nail on the head. I can see the bottle with that strap line. Maybe with something about its origin on Arran too.'

'Yes, that would be great.'

Carole produced an artist's pad. It was large. She placed it on her desk. She opened a packet of pastels and began to draw.

The words began to appear: Seaweed in My Hair Shampoo. Underneath she had located the origin of the seaweed. (From the shores of Arran, Scotland.) She drew bottles, tins, and tubes with the same design.

'That's a start. Now the Boots scientists will start on the production. Are you able to supply regular amounts of seaweed?'

'Yes, it's abundant. But how will I send it?'

'You don't. We send a lorry when you have a lorry full. Does that make sense?'

'I suppose so. So do I let you know when I have a large amount?'

'No Alec will be your contact. There are different van sizes. I'll give you his e-mail.' She opened her desk drawer. 'And here's my card if you want to discuss anything else.'

'It seems so simple,' said Kate.

'Lots more to do before we launch it. We have to set pricing. As the supplier and instigator of this venture, you receive 10% on every sale. We'll have magazine and TV launches and hope to film you on Arran collecting the seaweed. You up for that?'

'I certainly am. Gosh, I had no idea this was possible.'

'You are right of course, selling any seaweed product is not a new idea but it is a market which has not really got off the ground. We have high hopes for this project. You will make a lot of money through this, you realise?'

Kate's eyes opened wide and a smile shone though. Then she seemed to have a thought in mind. 'You know this would never have happened at Nuthatch. I had to be on Arran to make it happen.'

'That's how things work. Serendipity I'd say.'

'Naval contacts too,' said Kate and they both stood up to shake hands on the deal.

At 2 pm they parted with their cases and took a taxi to Heathrow. Two and a half hours later they landed in Glasgow by which time Bruce had heard about the contract to supply seaweed and the 10% deal.

They arrived home late, having stopped in Brodick for tea at the Cruze bar Brassiere where Cannelloni was chosen by Kate and a seafood Pizza satisfied Bruce. The light was fading when Kate was dropped off at her home. There was a letter lying on the hall carpet. She thought she'd read it the following morning as she felt tired. But the letter had the Police Scotland logo on the back. She tore it open and pulled out the one-page letter.

It was from Sergeant Murdoch. It revealed only two sentences.'I thought I should keep you informed. Mullard Davies was sentenced to twenty-eight years as a prison sentence for the double child murders.'

Kate clutched the letter close to her. She felt a weight off her shoulders had just taken place. She went to bed with a sense of resolution and of calmness. Her life was taking on good shape, at long last.

21

It was the local school children that responded to Kate's request for seaweed gatherers. It enhanced their pocket money amid fresh sea air and their parents were grateful to Kate as it removed them from their games consoles and iPads.

Kate parked both her car and the van outside on the patch of ground opposite her house, making the garage free to gather and dry the seaweed. After three weeks the first lorry arrived to take the seaweed to London. Kate was very pleased and recorded the uptake on camera with a host of the seaweed gathering school children.

Being business savvy more than ever, Kate contacted Hugh Boag once more.

'I'm sending you a photograph of the first delivery of seaweed to Boots in London. They are starting off with a series of Arran seaweed products under the brand name Seaweed in My Hair.'

'That's fantastic,' Hugh said.

'Local employment too. Schoolchildren gather the seaweed after school and they are supervised by two mothers,' informed Kate.

'But won't the seaweed eventually be finished and create an eco-imbalance if not a disaster for sea creatures,' asked Hugh.

'That's the beauty of seaweed. What is collected is shore seaweed. Great seaweed fields lie under deeper water and what is taken is quickly replenished naturally.'

'I see. Will you be concentrating in one area only?'

'No, all around Arran there is seaweed. School children can collect it anywhere and we'll bag it up for London.'

'Is it only school children that can gather the seaweed?'

'No Hugh, the elderly can if they are able and any unemployed person seeking work can apply. This is very much an Arran product.'

Before long a photographer came to take Kate's photo along with her seaweed gathering children. That was soon made into a TV advert with the music of One Direction to accompany the broadcasts. Adverts were placed in several colour magazines as well as the weekend papers.

Kate was very busy with her hairdressing in the morning, now finishing at 1 pm each day. She organised the school children's weekly fees and gathered and sorted the seaweed. Once a fortnight on a Friday, she would go around the island to the seaweed delivery points and Alec in London was kept informed to arrange lorry deliveries.

It wasn't long before Boots stocked The Seaweed in My Hair products. By October Hair Shampoos;

Toothpaste; Cosmetics ranges and Skincare were on sale under the brand name with "From the shores of Arran, Scotland" shown prominently displayed on each product. Kate made sure all chemists and superstores on Arran sold the products and Bruce was as pleased, as she was, to see the line take off.

In her mail, one October morning was a more formal letter from David Tagg. She recognised his logo. Before she opened it the telephone rang. It was Bruce.

'Darling, I am very busy but I will phone you in ten minutes, okay,' she said.

'But if you are very busy won't you need more time?' asked Bruce.

Kate hesitated.

'Are you all right, dear?' he enquired.

'Why don't you come round in ten minutes then?'

'Well, if you are sure?'

'Yes, I might need a shoulder to cry on.'

'That sounds serious.'

Kate switched off her phone and took out a kitchen knife. She sliced open the letter and pulled out two ivory sheets of paper. She read the first formal sheet from the court with its formal conclusion, then the covering letter.

She put the letter back on the table and punched the air. The court recognised the irreconcilable breakdown of the marriage between Kate and Greg Bailey. She was officially divorced.

Bruce arrived fifteen minutes later with a bunch of cut Irises. Kate hugged Bruce and kissed him.

'Well, what was that all about? First, you were too busy, now you seem relaxed.'

She lifted her envelope. 'When you rang I was about to open this letter. Here read it.'

Bruce took the letter. He seemed suspicious. He saw the logo and looked serious. Kate's face gave nothing away. Then she found a vase filled it with water and placed his flowers in it. She brought them into the lounge.

Bruce returned the letter to the table and approached Kate. He squeezed her with his broad arms. 'That's wonderful news. Simply wonderful,' he said amid numerous kisses.

Morag Ritchie knocked on Kate's door one morning before she set off to cut the hair of the Machrie community.

'Good morning. I'm Morag Ritchie. I am looking for part-time work. I work with my sister-in-law at her wee shop. We are not making enough money for two salaries...... I trained as a hairdresser and wondered if you needed a hand?'

'Come in,' said a smiling Kate wondering if this might be an interesting development. She had to think quickly. Was her seaweed harvesting viable as a full-time job? Could she adapt the van to have two chairs; what did part-time mean? 'Shall we have a coffee?'

'Thank you. Tea if you don't mind,' said Morag.

'Yes, let me make a pot. I'll have tea for a change too,' she said clicking the kettle to boil.

'I hear you were a Chelsea hairstylist before. You obviously have a lot of experience.'

'The word has got around,' Kate replied.

'You cut my aunt's hair at Pirnmill and she told me all about your venture.'

'Yes, clients seem very friendly. I've got to know many.'

'I like the idea of a mobile hairdresser,' Morag said crossing her legs and flicking a spot of dust from her lap.

'Do you have a driving licence?'

'Yes, current with no points on it,' she said realising she had not brought it with her.

'Let's go out to the van and you'll see what I have.'

Kate liked Morag's buoyant personality and her smart appearance. The idea of a partner was growing in her mind.

'This is the setup,' she said as the cupboards were opened to reveal scissors, curlers, heating tongs, hairdryer, straighteners, and rings.

'How long have you been a hairdresser?'

'I was with Click Click in Sauchiehall Street for six years. Then I married and came to Arran with my husband. It's his sister I work for but as I say, it does not pay well.'

'What about driving the van, if you were on your own?'

'My husband, Alec, drives a grocer's van. I've driven that too. It's about the size of this.'

'And if you were alone in the van and an incident took place...'

'You mean like a robbery? No problem. We had a few till snatchers in Glasgow city centre. We caught a few ourselves.'

'So you could manage, it seems.'

'Yes, but the island is not full of Glaswegian gangsters. In fact, there's not much point in crime on the island. It's an island after all.'

Kate resisted a nod recalling her experience. But that was fast fading on her mind. She liked Morag and there and then appointed her to work for her. She suggested that she work Mondays, Tuesdays, and Thursdays.

'I am becoming increasingly busy with the Seaweed in My Hair line so I can see you taking over in due course. Would you be interested in going full-time eventually, providing we both agree on terms?'

'If you are pleased with my work, then I'd love to work five days a week.'

'We'll see how it goes. Now pay. I can pay you £10 per hour with you taking all the tips from your own clients. How does that sound?'

'Much better than I'm earning at present.'

So Morag began working three days a week and Kate received glowing reports. Her monthly cheques from Boots and the other outlets ticked over and soon Morag was working four days a week. Having one day a week kept Kate in touch with her rural communities. Thursdays were her day off and to the golf course she went for a morning's round. In the afternoon, her business hat was on and she kept a steady flow of dry raw seaweed on the road to London.

One Friday afternoon after a post-golf shower, a freshly spruced Kate came down to the lounge. A police car drew up outside her front door and she noticed Sergeant Rory Murdoch close his car door. She went to the front door to welcome him in.

'Sergeant, it's good to see you. Dropping in socially?' she asked with a generous smile on her face. Sergeant Murdoch did not share the smile.

'May I come in?'

Of course. You know where the lounge is.'

Kate detected aloofness. A business-type approach was called for.

'Kate, I have some news you must be aware of as it may have consequences for you.'

'Do I need a lawyer?' she asked instinctively.

'No, not yet. We will just have to see how the case develops. It is about Mullard Davies.'

'Mullard Davies, but he received a long prison sentence,' Kate said with confidence. 'He's out of the way, surely?'

'Let me tell you what happened. First, of course, Davies always denied any knowledge of the deaths of the two young children. Just before his verdict, the Crown Prosecution Service in Wales received information that Colin Edwards admitted the murder of his step-daughter Abigail Jones and her friend Lin Owens. Mullard Davies' defence counsel immediately filed for an appeal against his conviction because the Crown Prosecution Service failed to inform the defence of this development. As someone else had been charged with the same murders, his client was innocent, his conviction unsafe and he had to be released. That's what happened last Thursday,' Sergeant Murdoch said, then looked up from his prepared statement.

'Well, he's an innocent man after all. He should not be in prison for a crime he did not commit. So how does this involve me?'

Sergeant Murdoch shook his head and sighed. 'He was re-arrested on Friday and taken to Ayr. 'On Monday he made his first appearance and was detained pending trial on account of your intended rape, theft of money, possession of an offensive weapon, and theft of a motorbike. And this is where you come in. He denies the charges.'

21

Bruce learned of the recent events over an evening meal at Kate's home the following day.

'Cheers.' Bruce raised his glass.

'Here's to Mullard admitting his offences against me,' said Kate clicking her wine glass with his.

'I can't see him denying your case. Yours is watertight, in my view,' he said tapping her forearm in a sympathetic gesture.

'Bruce, I thought his Welsh murders were watertight but they weren't.'

'So, Sergeant Murdoch said he denied the offences? But a good solicitor who is dealing with him would tell him admitting an offence carries a lighter sentence.'

'So that would mean I'd not be called?'

'It would mean you would not be served a citation.'

Kate reflected on Bruce's words. It did seem more likely he'd accept his guilt. 'But he is up on four charges remember?'

'Lawyers often make deals. The attempted rape is the main charge so a fiscal might drop the other charges.'

'That doesn't seem fair,' said Kate perplexed.

'Anyway, we can wait and see how that materialises.'

Kate brought through the steak pie and began to serve it.

'Mmm.. looks and smells good.'

Bruce served the roast potatoes. 'So how is Morag getting on?'

Kate smiled at Bruce. 'I'm glad she called here. It makes my double work easier.'

'Yes, I'm thinking about that. It's difficult to have two professions,' he said in a serious tone.

'Two professions indeed. You make it sound so important,' she laughed. 'I'm a hairdresser who gathers seaweed.'

Hang on. Don't put yourself down. Don't forget you are the managing director of Seaweed in My Hair. You have the rights and the dividends coming in as you told me. It's what a good manager earns. You could sell the hair van and work entirely with the seaweed.'

'I'd miss meeting people, creating hairstyles, and managing their hair care. I suppose it's all about getting the balance right.'

Bruce put his knife and fork down and looked straight across the table at Kate. 'Can I add one more matter into the mix?' he said with an impish grin.

Kate had no idea what he had in mind. She found her eyebrows raised.

Bruce took the salt cellar and placed it at the end of the table. Then he took the pepper pot and placed it halfway down the table. He pointed at the salt. 'That's where I live.' Then he pointed to the pepper pot. 'That's where you live. It is a pleasant walk in spring, summer, and autumn to our houses but not so pleasant in winter. You agree?'

'Hard not to disagree,' she said with an inkling of what he was about to say and it made her feel on edge.

'Now here's me as a ninety-five-year-old walking to your house,' he said as he used two walking fingers to move very slowly. 'Now the question arises, why is he so old and still walking to see you?'

'Because we'd be in love still?'

'Exactly. However, I have a solution. I'll explain after coffee.'

'You are teasing me, Bruce.'

The bread and butter pudding was superb with just the right amount of sultanas. Bruce finished his plate quickly but Kate's stomach was floating in a spin. Vague anticipation always made her feel that way.

'I'll fix the coffee,' said Bruce heading off into the kitchen.

That gave Kate a chance to finish her pudding in a sedate lonely manner.

POP

'Are you all right?' asked a concerned Kate.

'Everything is under control. Coffee coming up soon. I'll be through shortly. Don't you come in.'

Kate put both arms behind her head and took a deep breath. Was she right to prepare herself this way? Then Bruce came in holding two coffees. 'There we are. Here's your coffee and here's mine.' Bruce sat down and raised his coffee to his lips. 'Too hot,' he said and got up from the table.

He came round and stood beside Kate. Then he dropped down onto one knee. Kate took a deep sigh of delight and anticipation.

'Kate, you came into my life just over four months ago. We began on the golf course and have since then gone into business had fun and had lots of ups and a very few downs. But in all we've done together, I've never been as happy in my life. You have made me so complete, that ....I.... (he struggled to extract the box from his back pocket) ...I....want to share the rest of my life with you. Kate darling, will you be my wife? Will you marry me?'

Kate stood up and helped Bruce rise. He placed the engagement ring on her finger. Kate grabbed his face with both of her hands and drew him to her kisses amid which she replied. 'Of course, I'll marry you, darling.'

After a series of hugs and kisses, Bruce returned to the kitchen and brought out two glasses of champagne. They clicked their glasses wishing each other love and happiness then Kate looked in horror. The dining room curtains had not been drawn and two couples were clapping outside.

Bruce waved his arm at them inviting them in and they arrived with an active spaniel whose walk had taken an interesting turn. They shared a glass of Champaign wishing the couple happiness and Bruce knew that the new arrivals would inform the village of the evening's event quicker than a greyhound chasing a rabbit.

After their visitors had left, Kate returned to the salt and pepper theme. 'So where is home for us?'

'I'm much attached to my family home and of course, it has a good-sized garden for a growing family. Yet I admit the sea view is more restricted.'

'I hoped you would say that. Much as I love this house, it really belongs to the Zaidis. If I put the house on the market, I'd hope to get the buying price and I'd return the money to them. You agree?'

'Of course. Their money served its purpose.'

'Indeed. Now to the dishes. I'll wash and you dry, fiancé.'

22

The garage was full once more and so the call went out to London. Kate chided herself for not taking sufficient account of the numerous shores where the local children were harvesting seaweed. Contented parents brought their damp vegetation to her in Blackwaterfoot regularly. The children always welcomed their extra pocket money too.

It was a somewhat haphazard delivery at times and hence the garage was almost too full. It was also now November and after-school hours were dark. Nevertheless, it did not seem to detract from sales which had now gone to Boots 3,063 worldwide stores and Boots 2,465 stores in the UK.

In a report from London, Kate read in the British section, that toothpaste was ticking over well as a product bought every three months but the shampoo was flying off the shelves especially in the southeast and southwest of England. Ointments and balms were next in line but generally, the advertising had paid off and the public at large had Seaweed in My Hair and on their minds. Kate was anxious to see how Arran did with sales but was disappointed to read their local results were swallowed by a whole of Scotland report in which it also gave glowing reports.

Her business overcame the gloom of the end of the year. Her telescope gave her fewer hours to engage in spying boats, people on Kintyre and sea mammals, and ocean-going sea birds.

It was on one such miserably dull Saturday morning before she set out to shop, the postman arrived. He did not stay long. His delivery did not flop onto the hall floor. Rather it slid along the linoleum like a taxiing aeroplane coming to a halt near the kitchen door. She smiled at its final journey until she recognised the formality of the envelope. She picked it up. It had been sent from the Crown Office, Procurator Fiscal Service at Ayr. She sliced the letter open.

It was a citation from the Procurator Fiscal for Kate Bailey to attend the Sheriff court at Ayr on 27th November, at 10 am, as a witness for the prosecution in the case of Mullard Davies. The charges being attempted rape, theft of money and a motorbike, and possession of an offensive weapon, namely a pen knife.

As a witness from Arran, the Fiscal gave her a telephone number and an e-mail for her to be contacted if there was no sailing on the day. Taxi fares from Ardrossan to the court at Ayr and back would be reimbursed. That seemed little comfort. She had no wish to see Mullard Davies again.

'Bruce dear, I've received the citation.'

'Hi, well perhaps as expected. It still does not mean having to give evidence.'

'It looks like it to me,' she said drumming the fingers of her left hand on the table.

'So when is the court date?'

'27th November at 10 am.'

'Let me see....here it is. It's a Monday morning. So why not let's go up to Ayr on Sunday, stay overnight, and then you'll be fresh for court in the morning?'

'You'll be a great support. Yup. Can I leave you to find a place to stay?'

'Sure. Heard of the Brig o' Doon House hotel in Alloway?'

'No, don't think so.'

'Well, if we can get a room, you'll be impressed.'

A delighted Kate was piped into the hotel by a young piper the day before the trial. Their room overlooked the hotel gardens at the back and just beyond was the actual Bridge of Doon where Robert Burns crossed on many an occasion. Kate was in Burns country.

That night they ate in the main restaurant but Kate took no wine. She required a clear head in the morning.

The bedroom was warm, the heavy curtains pulled close and the carpet's pile so deep not a sound could be heard as they undressed. With pyjamas still under their pillows they entered the fresh hotel sheets and their naked bodies hugged one another. Bruce ran his fingers through Kate's hair and she let out a quiet whimper. His hands slipped down to her breasts and he held them firmly at first then massages them until their nipples stood to attention.

Bruce turned to lie on top of his fiancée and directed his manhood to its rightful place and as he thrust, Kate realised she was in a fertile phase. It was not the time to mention this, she knew. It was time to enjoy the closeness of a life's partner where two bodies' couple and sheer bliss were shared. At the completion of the union, Bruce rolled over and within moments he was fast asleep. Kate got out of bed and set the alarm for 7 am.

Breakfast was downstairs in an area close to the back garden. Being late November there were no flowers to see but the lawn had been immaculately manicured and any fallen leaves swept out of sight. A robin jumped onto a nearby fence as they ate. Bruce had the full Scottish breakfast and tucked into the haggis, dipping it into a fried egg. They both drank tea. Kate put her knife and fork down. The Scottish smoked salmon slice with lemon sauce was too rich she felt. She put her plate to one side and selected a slice of toast from the wrack. No sooner had she done that, her plate was taken away.

At 9:25 they ordered a taxi and it arrived six minutes later. It brought them to Wellington Square and the Sheriff Court house at Ayr.

Kate reported to the desk on arrival. She was ushered to a waiting room. Bruce was instructed to sit in the public viewing gallery at Court number 2. At 10 am precisely, the fifteen members of the jury filed into their appointed rows of seating. Bruce did not recognise any of them but felt the two ladies in twin suits with blue rinses were almost certain to convict an attempted rapist. There was a younger man, about twenty-five perhaps. He seemed to be overcome by the occasion and his eyes flitted around the court like a bee trying to find an open window. The fifteen jurors, in every other way, just looked like people you'd encounter on a double-decker bus.

'Court rise,' shouted the ex-army sergeant major court official and the black gowned Sheriff Alex Miller took to his lofted position above the well of the court.

The jury was appointed appropriately without fuss.

'Yes,' was all the sheriff said and the Procurator Fiscal, Ms. Gwen Clark stood to introduce the case.

'M' Lord, this is a case of attempted rape, theft of money and a motorbike, and possession of an offensive weapon. All four charges are on the same indictment,' she stated and sat down promptly.

Gordon Hodge stood as Mullard Davies' legal counsel and offered no objection.

'Very well, Ms. Clark?'

Gwen got to her feet once more and Bruce sat on the edge of his seat expecting his fiancée to be summonsed.

'I call upon Sergeant Rory Murdoch,' she said and smiled at him when he entered the court. He took the oath, then returned the Bible to the court usher.

'Tell the court your name, age, and length of police service, officer please.'

'I am Sergeant Rory Murdoch aged 35 and have had fifteen years service in Police Scotland.'

'Objection, ma lord,' shouted Gordon Hodge.

Sheriff Miller stared daggers fearing a multitude of irrelevant objections might prolong the case and frustrate the fiscal. 'Yes,' he said sharply.

'Your witness, a police officer, tells the court he has been a police officer with Police Scotland for fifteen years. Police Scotland is less than ten years old,' he remarked and sat down.

'How pedantic Mr. Hodge. I take it that the officer has served the police for fifteen years and you know that as well as everyone else in the court this morning. I warn you, I will not tolerate any other flippant objections,' warned Sheriff Miller.

There was a silence that spread around the courtroom like wildfire. The rules seemed set. Despite the solemnity of the moment, Greg smiled. To him, it was 1-0 for the prosecution. The sheriff had scored the first goal.

'Officer, can you identify Mr. Mullard Davies?'

'Yes, that's him there, seated over there,' he pointed to him.

'Officer, you are based at Lamlash on Arran. Can you tell the court what happened on June 16th this year?'

'I was on mobile patrol at Kirkpatrick when I received a distressed call from a woman, Miss Kate

Bailey. She was at the time being comforted by Rev Colin Craig.'

'What were your findings?'

'When I arrived at the scene, on the main road, I parked behind the minister's car and found a young woman with a torn blouse and out of breath.'

'What did she tell you?'

'That a man, a Welshman, had taken money from her haircutting takings then tried to rape her.'

'Objection,' said Mr. Hodge once more.

'Very well,' said the sheriff.

'No evidence has been shown to say he was Welsh.'

'Mr. Hodge. That is not an objection. The woman thought he was Welsh because she must have heard, to her ear, a Welsh accent. He is either Welsh or not. I thought you might have ascertained such a simple fact yourself, or are you telling the court your client is not Welsh?' asked the Sheriff pursing angry lips.

Mr. Hodge looked sheepish and did not reply.

Gwen returned to her feet. 'After your initial conversation with Miss Bailey, what happened next?'

'We returned to her mobile hairdressing van where the alleged theft and attempted rape took place.'

'My lord, I am sure the officer meant the alleged theft and the alleged attempted rape. Both are alleged offences and remain so, at present.'

Gwen threw her eyes to the ceiling.

'Point taken. Pedantic Mr. Hodge, pedantic,' said the Sheriff.

'Officer, now tell the court what you saw in the van.'

'I was shown the drawer from which Miss Bailey handed over the money.'

'Objection again. Exactly M'lord. Handed over the money. I need this noted. On her own volition, it can be surmised, she handed over the money voluntarily.'

'We shall hear before too long, I suspect,' said the canny Sheriff.

Murdoch continued. 'I also took a sample of red hair from the premises and had it analysed. There was also a semen sample taken from the van floor. The semen matched the hair.'

'I submit the said DNA report from Dr. Gordon Eccles as Production 1, M'lord,' said Gwen passing the report over to Mr. Hodge. 'It shows a match of DNA similarity in both semen and hair.'

The sheriff noted it as being lodged.

'Did Mr. Davies come to your attention at a later date, officer' asked Gwen.

'Yes, I received a telephone call from a Mrs. Anne Baxter who found a motorbike abandoned near her home at Corrie. This motorbike had been stolen the previous day from Lochranza. The owner reported that man of Mr. Davies' description stole his motorbike.'

'I have no further questions to ask the officer,' said Gwen sitting down and preparing a fresh sheet of her notebook.

Mr. Hodge got to his feet. 'Just a couple of points to clarify. Officer, you said the hair was red. Look at my client. He is as blond and clean-shaven almost like the day he was born. I put it to you that this so-called red hair was from one of Miss Bailey's earlier female customers?'

'Possible, I admit but his hair was analysed.....' but Sergeant Murdoch could not complete his sentence.

'Thank you, Mr. Murdoch,' said Gordon Hodge turning his back on the witness and sitting down. 'Thank you, Constable, you may stand down now.

My next witness is the Reverend Mr. Colin Craig.'

Bruce wondered why Kate's evidence was being delayed but there again he had no idea of the workings of the Crown's case.

'Please tell the court your name, age, and profession.'

'I am Colin Craig aged fifty-three and a Church of Scotland minister at St Molios Church at Blackwaterfoot.'

'And how long have you been minister of that church?'

'For the past four years, I was in Hamilton before that.'

'Now let me take you back to the events of 16th June. What were you doing that afternoon?'

'I was travelling to visit one of my elderly members to deliver the sacrament of Holy Communion at her home in Pirnmill.'

'But you were delayed, not so?'

'Yes, I was around a mile or two outside the village of Pirnmill when I saw a young lady in the middle of the road.'

'What action did you take?'

'I slowed down and parked at the side of the road and found the young woman to be distressed.'

'In what way distressed?'

'Well her blouse had been badly torn, her hair was unkempt and she was sweating profusely.'

'My lord production number 2. The torn blouse,' said Gwen placing the garment on the table for all to see. 'I ask you to note the report by the forensic scientist Dr. Laura Spiers, which accompanies this garment. She writes that the tear on both sides of the garment could only have come from a two-handed simultaneous rip.' Then she returned to question the minister.

'What did you do next?'

'She asked if I had a mobile phone, so I gave it to her but her hands were shaking so much she asked me to phone 999.'

'And did you?'

'Yes, that was when Sergeant Rory Murdoch came to tend to Miss Bailey.'

'Objection. How did the minister know her name?' asked Gordon Hodge.

'Well, she told me. And everyone knows Miss Bailey. She is the managing director of Seaweed in My Hair. You have heard of them, haven't you?' asked the minister.

Mr. Hodge may have visited Boots for his shaving requirements however Seaweed in My Hair caught him off balance and he failed to capitalise on his instinct.

'One final question, M'lord. The good minister has not been able to identify my client.' And he sat down smugly.

'M'lord, I did not require the minister's identification. I knew the Reverend Mr. Craig had never encountered the accused,' said Gwen Clark confidently.

'Objection dismissed. Quite irrelevant Mr. Hodge and I for one am getting tired of your jack-in-the-box objections,' the wise sheriff said mopping his brow.

Then as Bruce was wondering about his missed 11 o'clock coffee, her name was called and Kate appeared in the witness box. Nervously she took the oath.

'Please tell the court your full name, age, and profession asked Gwen in a perfunctory manner.

'My name is Kate Murray Ann Bailey. I am thirty-three years of age and I am the managing director of Seaweed in My Hair.'

'Look around the court. Do you see the man alleged to have attempted to rape you?'

'Yes, that's him there.' She pointed confidently and then looked away in disgust.

'In your own words tell the court what happened on 16th June this year?' asked Gwen.

'I arrived on Arran on 6th June and on 16th set off on my first mobile hairdressing appointments.'

'Do you recall whose hair you cut that day?'

'You mean the ladies' hair?'

'Yes, all the heads you cut that day.'

Kate hesitated. She wondered what the procedure would be. 'Err,' she said as she opened her handbag and brought out a diary. 'I have all the names in my diary. Let me see..'

'Miss Bailey, the names in your diary were they written on the actual days, or is this a record you have made of your clients since?' asked the Sheriff.

'I'm looking at 16th June only, that's when I wrote their names. It will help me to remember them.'

'I see, carry on,' invited the Sheriff.

'I had four customers that day. Mrs. Barker had a blue rinse colouring to her hair. I cut her hair and shaped it as well. Mrs. Graham and Mrs. McGregor both have white hair and they each received the same procedure as Mrs. Barker. Miss Reid has short black hair. I washed hers and layered her hair.'

'You are sure none had red hair?'

'I am definitely sure. I would not lie.'

'Of course not. So, after you had finished with your clients, what happened,' asked Gwen.

'A man approached the van a little out of breath. This man sitting there,' she pointed. 'He had wild red hair and a red beard too, he was......

'M'lord,' interrupted Mr. Hodge, 'the statement of the hairdresser was that her alleged attacker had wild red hair. I invite you to look at the near blond hair my client sports. Not a trace of red about it. He's not a Manchester United supporter,' said Gordon Hodge with a grin following his sporting remark, then he sat down.

'I may be wrong but don't Welshmen support rugby and doesn't their national team play in red?' suggested Kate.

'Well observed,' smiled the Sheriff while Mr. Hodge stared daggers at Kate. Gwen smiled too at her opponent's comeuppance.

'May I bring you back to your first meeting with Mullard Davies? Please continue,' invited Gwen Clark.

'He entered the van and immediately took a seat. I asked what he wanted me to do and he told me to change his hair colouring. As I took the scissors to his hair I noticed he was not a natural red-head but he had had a henna treatment and his roots were much darker, mousy dark. Anyway, he asked me to shave off his beard and give him a blond look. It was when he had finished that he brought out a penknife and threatened me. He asked for my day's takings and I opened the drawer and gave him all the notes. When I handed the money over, he grabbed me around my waist trapping my arms, and began to kiss me. I tried to turn away. His intentions were clear and so I remembered what my former husband had told me what to do in these dire moments. I pretended to cooperate with him and told him I had condoms in the van. He eased off me and I went to a drawer near the door where I knew I had a toilet bag. I lifted the bag telling him there were several condoms in it but when I turned around he had lowered his trousers and exposed himself at me.'

'M'lord, unsupported evidence and flatly denied by my client,' said Gordon Hodge and promptly sat down.

'It is the nature of the alleged attack, Mr. Hodge. Your time will come to cross-examine,' said the Sheriff.

'I observed that Mr. Davies had a brown mole on the shaft of his penis. I saw it clearly because I then kicked as hard as I could at his testicles. That's when he fell down and I escaped by running up the road where I met the vicar.'

'Minister, Miss Bailey, you are not in England now,' informed the Sheriff.

'Yes, the minister, sorry. Then Sergeant Murdoch arrived and we went back to the van. That's when he saw all the red hair I had cut and I told him it was from the man who tried to rape me. He bagged some and said he'd get it analysed. A DNA sample he said.'

'Thank you, Miss Bailey,' said Gwen then she looked at Mr. Hodge.

'My lord, just a couple of points if I may in cross-examination. Miss Bailey, what state of attire were you in when my client was having his hair cut?'

'My usual hair dressers' clothes.'

'Create a picture of them in my mind, if you please.'

'I wore a blouse, that blouse on the table, and a skirt, knee length.'

'And the neckline of the blouse, a V shape or high at the neck, you know perhaps a turtle neck?'

'No, it was not high at the neck. A V-shaped blouse as you can see.'

'Indeed I can. A revealing V-shaped front and you cut my client's hair and shaved him. Just imagine being in front of my client bending over to shave him or cutting his hair from the front, now was that not an invitation to be seductive?'

Bruce felt rage. Oh, how he would have loved to knock that solicitor to the ground. He hoped the questioning of his fiancée would soon be over.

'When I cut his hair, I was behind him. When I shaved him, his head was back and the blade sharp. There was no provocation. None whatsoever.'

'My final point. What did the Sergeant tell you about my client?'

'Er... I can't remember,' Kate said.

'If I mention the word Murder, does that ring a bell?'

'Ah yes. That he was to be tried for the double murder of two young children in Wales?'

The gallery drew in their breath in unison.

Mr. Hodge nodded and took his time to pace up and down the jury rows. 'And did you know my client was cleared of these two charges? He did not commit any murders.'

'Yes, I learned another man committed the murders,' she replied.

'Exactly, he was just a man seeking a new future on a quiet peace-loving island hoping to find some work and some love. Words I could have said about you too. It's a pity you did not meet on more favourable terms. I have no further questions.'

Bruce was outraged by the trickery of this defence lawyer. He was anxious to get to Kate and give her a comforting hug. That moment would arrive soon.

'I have no other witnesses,' said Gwen.

'Mr. Hodge? Have you?' asked the sheriff.

'Yes, just one witness, my client.'

'Then I feel we should adjourn for lunch and resume the case at 2 pm.'

'Court Rise,' bellowed the court official.

23

The Fox and Willow on Carrick Road was where they managed to have lunch. Bruce was ready for a heavy meal but Kate was still recovering from her ordeal in both remembering what happened on 16th June and from the jibes from Mr. Hodge. She chose a tuna salad. Bruce went for a plate of fish and chips with mushy peas.

'So part of you is Scottish,' said Bruce.

'And which part is that?' she replied.

'Please state your full name Kate Murray Ann Bailey. I rest my case m'lord,' he laughed.

'I almost forgot too yes, my grandfather on my mother's side was a Murray but I don't know where from in Scotland. I've never really studied our family tree,' she admitted.

Kate drank a glass of Sprite. 'I think only a certain type of personality could be a defence lawyer,' she said.

'Much better to be a fiscal.'

'Yes, Gwen is nice.'

'You know we could go home now. Your performance is over,' said Bruce.

'Yes we could but I want to see how Mullard Davies acts in court. I can't see him getting out of this. Can you?'

'I suspect he's about to dig a hole for himself.'

At 1:55 Bruce and Kate were in the public gallery ready for the afternoon performance. Gwen and Mr. Hodge were close together taking notes. They separated abruptly as the sheriff took to his chair.

Mr. Hodge was first to stand. 'My Lord, my client wishes to accept two of the charges. Namely, that he carried a penknife, a closed penknife in his pocket, and was in possession of the same. Secondly, he did steal the motorbike and abandoned it, in the village of Corrie. I think my friend, the fiscal, will agree to these accepted charges.'

'Mr. Hodge, surely I don't have to teach you to suck eggs. Your client had a penknife. Full Stop. Carrying a penknife in a pocket would not have come to light. As soon as the penknife is exposed in these criminal proceedings, that knife becomes an offensive weapon. That is what your client is admitting to, I assume?' asked the sheriff.

'Yes M'lord,' said Mr. Hodge who then sat down.

'Madam Prosecutor you accept both charges admitted.'

'Yes I do, noted, M'lord.'

'Then let us proceed on the remaining two charges, namely; the theft of money from the van and the attempted rape. Thank you.' said the sheriff.

'You are Mullard Davies and although you were born in Wales, you have not lived there for a long time, have you?' asked Gordon Hodge his solicitor.

'No, I've been away for a long while,' he replied in an obviously rich Welsh accent.

'So why did you move to Arran?'

'I like islands, Scottish islands. The people accept you more easily in these places,' Mullard said.

'But you were not visiting were you, I mean; you hoped to settle down on Arran, not so?'

'Yes, find the right woman, get a good job and settle down, as you say. That's what I wanted, more than anything else in the world.'

'Tell me what happened on 16th June. Take your time.'

'I needed a haircut badly. I was out on the road and I saw this van. When I got nearer I saw it was a hairdresser's mobile shop. I knocked on the van door. I was let in. She cut my hair and shaved my beard just what I wanted.'

'Now we heard you have accepted that you had a knife. Why did you bring it out?'

Kate sat forward, eager to hear more of his evidence.

'It's not really a knife. It's a pen knife with a small blade. I use it to clean my nails. That's what I was going to do. I guess it frightened her into thinking I was robbing her. That's when she gave me the money and I thought, that was very kind of her, so I showed my appreciation with a hug.'

'What happened next?'

'She relaxed, and I knew we could make a couple, so I asked if she was interested in having sex. She went to get condoms. I thought my life was on the mend. But she returned and kicked me hard, on the balls. I collapsed still wondering why she'd do that to me. I thought she liked me.'

'I have no further questions,' said Mr. Hodge and Gwen got to her feet.

'His evidence is a story, no more than that. I hope the jury doesn't believe him,' whispered Kate into Bruce's ear.

'Mr. Davies, so it was a romantic encounter in your evidence. Would that be fair to say?'

'Yes. Ma'am. It was certainly that, nothing else.'

'You see Production 1 on the table. A torn blouse. Was that the blouse Miss Bailey wore?'

'Yes, I think so.'

'So how did it get torn?'

'Err ...I think she got it torn on something. Maybe she turned too quickly, there's not much room in a hairdresser's van, you know.'

'I remind you of the forensic scientist's report on the tear. It was two hands that ripped the blouse. I can't see Kate Bailey ripping her own blouse. Can you?'

'No, I don't think she ripped it herself,' he replied.

'I put it to you that you lusted after her and could not control your urges.'

Mullard thought through the question and was confused. His reply drew breaths of astonishment from the jurors as well as his solicitor. 'Yes that's right, lust, I suppose it was. Makes you lose control, a bit, doesn't it?' he asked rhetorically.

'Was that how Miss Bailey was responding too?'

'No, I don't think she had as much lust as I did, unfortunately.'

'Tell me where did you go after this incident?' asked Gwen warming to his ineptitude.

'I went into hiding...'

'Why?' she asked quickly to keep up the tempo.

'I didn't want to get caught.'

'Caught for doing what?'

But Mullard chose not to get deeper into the water. The question had been asked. Everyone had heard. But no answer came. His silence would condemn him.

'I have no further questions.'

'Then Miss Clark, I invite you to sum up,' said Sheriff Miller.

Gwen sorted out a few papers then addressed the court. 'There is no doubt that the accused has been identified both by the alleged victim and Sergeant Murdoch. We have heard two testaments about the money being handed over to Mr. Davies. I invite the jury to decide whether this was a kind gesture by Miss Bailey or the actions of a frightened woman at the other end of a knife blade to hand over the money. The money being the takings of her very first day as a mobile hairdresser on Arran.'

Gwen paused. She ran her fingers through her hair.

'And so to the attempted rape. The blouse before you, and you may see it closer if you wish, does not seem to have one tear as one might expect from being caught on an opening cupboard or some other domestic item, as the accused described. This blouse which we have identified as being the property of the victim was torn on both sides inviting Dr. Laura Spiers to conclude two strong hands seized the blouse and pulled it apart causing such tears as seen. And so to the consequences. Flight after the brave assault on the perpetrator, running hard until a car stopped to come to her aid. The Reverend Mr. Craig's evidence spoke of a terrified woman, one who could not hold a phone. Certainly not the actions of a jilted lover.'

Kate leant forward crossing her legs to hear the crucial summing up continue.

'Sergeant Murdoch's inspection of the hairdressing van gave us the DNA in the hair and sperm, of ... Mullard Davies.'

Mullard began to lose interest. His eyes floated around Court number 2 till he fixed them on Kate's face. She turned away from his gaze.

'You as a jury are asked to decide on proof beyond reasonable doubt. Now you might have some doubt in the evidence you have heard but I urge you to find

Mullard Davies guilty of theft of money from the hairdressing van and guilty of attempted rape of the van owner Mrs. Kate Bailey. You have already heard he has admitted to the theft of the motorcycle and the possession of an offensive weapon. Put together we have a very dangerous man indeed. I ask you to find Mullard Davies guilty of attempting to rape Mrs. Kate Bailey and the theft of her day's takings from the van. Thank you.'

'Mr. Hodge' invited the Sheriff.

'My friend is right. This case depends on reaching a decision based on whether there is reasonable doubt. Again I stress reasonable doubt. There is doubt. My client has made his case. A lonely man grateful to have had a haircut and sees a charming lady caring for him. Was it a mistake? Yes, almost certainly. If he could only claw back the hands of time. Thwarted. Yes, that's the word, thwarted in love, thwarted in luck but today he looks you, the jury, in the eye and asked surely you will not thwart his efforts to find contentment in his life? I urge you to find my client not guilty. I thank you.'

'Ladies and gentlemen of the jury you have heard the witnesses, seen the productions together with eminent reports from expert witnesses, and heard the submissions of both the Crown and the defence. You must now retire to make your verdict. Take as long as you require,' said Sheriff Miller.

24

As the public gallery emptied, Kate caught the eye of Gwen. She looked up and gave a wave and a wink. It seemed she was satisfied with her day's work.

Bruce and Kate walked from the court to the nearby seafront. In the distance, they could see the Sleeping Warrior of the Arran hills. Before them, on Ayr's golden beach, some dog walkers ran along behind their excited pets.

'Well, it's all over now, Kate.'

Kate clung onto Bruce's arm 'Almost, yes.'

'Let's get home. We'll hear the verdict one way or another,'

'You are right. Our day in Ayr is ended and I know where my heart belongs.'

'With me?' asked Bruce.

'Yes, with you and Arran.'

They began to walk back to their hotel to collect their cases when a man tapped Bruce on his back.

'Home and dry. They can't possibly not convict.'

'Hi, Hugh. But the Banner will have to wait for the result surely? You cannot second guess a jury,' said Bruce.

Hugh tapped his satchel. 'I have the report of the proceedings in here with two endings. So it's written.

Just need the result. Mind you he accepted two offences so my report is really almost ready for print.'

The taxi brought them back to Ardrossan where they spent an hour in the terminal before sailing over to Brodick in the darkness. Lights twinkled and grew larger as the ship made progress. Kate and Bruce ventured out on the deck where a sharp cold breeze rushed over their faces.

'You've got to say this is bracing. You can't get this weather in London.'

Kate hung close to Bruce. 'The sooner we get on dry land the better. I love islands but I'm not the best of sailors.'

Bruce gave her a final squeeze. 'That's enough. Let's go inside for a coffee.'

Breakfast was a lazy Tuesday affair. But a round of golf had been planned to put the trial to bed, but it had not.

On the third tee about halfway down the fairway, Kate's phone rang. She wondered whether to switch it off but she could not help but see who had rung. It was a number that rang no bell in her mind.

'Hi, is that Kate Bailey?'

'Yes, Kate here.'

'The estate agent gave me your number.'

Kate's eyebrows congregated. 'Oh, I see.'

'My husband and I have your brochure and wonder if we can mosey round to see your property at your convenience?'

'Ah, yes, of course. Where are you now?'

'We are enjoying a coffee at the Shiskine hotel. That is me, Debra, and my husband Larry.'

'We could be back in an hour? How does that suit you?'

'Sure suits us fine. An hour is just perfect. We'll take a wander along the beach after we leave here and see you at, let me see, 12:30 yes?'

'Yes, 12:30. Till then Debra, bye.'

Kate jumped up and down waving her number three iron. Bruce stopped to watch her antics then placed his fists on his hips. 'What's got into you?' he enquired.

'Two Americans want to see around the house. Game's over, I'd better get back home and tidy up.'

Kate just had enough time to have a quick shower and changed into casual wear before tidying up papers, and dishes. Bruce had already hoovered the downstairs carpets and was giving the windows a swipe. As his focus on the window changed to the movement approaching, he shouted to Kate. 'Here they are. They have an SUV with a bull bar. I think they must be Texans.' He set off to answer the door.

'Good morning. I'm Bruce my fiancée is Kate, she'll be here in a moment. Please come in.'

'Mighty pleased to do so, I'm Larry,' he said stretching out a large palm.

'I'm Debra.....'

'Come through to the lounge.'

'Gee honey, is that not a picture to draw?' Larry said as he looked through the window. He stood at the bay window tapping the telescope.

'Fantastic, ain't it honey?'

'Sure is.'

'So you are an artist?' Bruce asked out of interest.

'I sure dabble with the oils,' Debra replied.

'Arran's a long way from the USA,' said Bruce unable to think of anything else to say.'

'We've spent most of our working life in Scotland. Well, off Scotland. Oil of course. But it's time to retire and we thought, we got lots of friends in Scotland and few left in Seattle, Washington State where I'm from, or Florida where Larry's from. The weather's better here. Less extreme, and we love the sea and islands.'

'Blackwaterfoot has a small harbour,' added Bruce but they did not seem interested in sailing.

'I guess, if we are being frank. I've got ten years to live. I want to live these last few years on a quiet island, with villages not so far away, where I can wake to the westerly winds and see the choppy seas some mornings and a sea as calm as a glass window the next day.' Then Larry walked across the floor to greet Kate.

'Ma'am, you have a mighty fine home here. You sure you gonna give it up?' He asked extending his hand.

'Sell it, yes. I am engaged to Bruce and we have two houses.'

Larry smiled. 'I guess he's got the bigger house, then, yeah?'

'Yes, it is but it has history too. It's his family home.'

'Wow, history. We ain't got so much of that, back home.'

'Can we mosey around upstairs and see the rest of the house?'

'Sure. Come this way,' said Kate with a spring in her step.

Over the next hour and a quarter, the American couple cross-examined Bruce and Kate about the local people, where to buy things, and what they thought of the summers and winters at Blackwaterfoot. Naturally, they put a positive spin on the village and the island – in their eagerness to sell.

'That snooker table you got in the garage and the nearness of the golf course sells the house for me. Ideal situation too,' said Larry.

'Then put your wallet to your talk, Larry,' said a practical Debra.

'You selling for £260K?'

'Yes. And if we bought when would be the date of entry?'

'As soon as you wish. I have a home to go to,' Kate said looking at Bruce who confirmed what she had said.

'Then here's the deal. I've just turned 65 so I'll give you £265K if you promise not to sell to a different bidder.'

'Deal,' said Kate, offering her hand to shake. He took it firmly and shook it up and down with glee.

'We don't gazump in Scotland, the handshake seals the deal. I'll let you confirm that with the estate agents,' said Bruce amazed at his faulty generosity.

'Can I ask where you are staying at present?'

'Sure, Kate. We are staying with an old oil worker's family at Lamlash. We can be there another week or so.'

'Then as soon as we get the green light from the agents, the house is yours. We should be able to clear out in four days,' added Bruce.

'So, Saturday change-over day?' Larry confirmed.

And they shook hands over that too.

When the Americans set off, Bruce and Kate high-fived each other. A very quick sale, a considerable profit, and four hectic days to clear out the Seaweed business from Kate's home to Bruce's double garage. They had their hands full. They had never worked so hard with Bruce putting off his writing and Kate putting aside her hairdressing business.

Morag took on the hairdressing full time during this period and she soon had the client numbers growing.

On Wednesday afternoon the phone rang. It was Hugh Boag from the Banner. 'Hi, Kate. You may not have heard the news. We've just received it. Mullard Davies was found guilty and is off to do a fourteen-year sentence at her majesty's pleasure, for attempted rape, theft of money and a motorbike, and carrying an offensive weapon. We are putting out the full story leading up to this morning's conviction. Arran folk have been following this one from the start.'

'That's great. The story is in good hands. Well not so much a story, as a dairy of real events, perhaps,' suggested Kate.

'There's another subject I want to bring to your attention.'

'Really?'

'Yes, you have been nominated for Arran's new businesswoman of the year.'

'Goodness, what does that involve?'

'A Gala evening at which sporting, community awards, and business awards take place in January. Good month for indoor events. It will be at the Ormidale Hotel, Brodick, in the glass conservatory. Mind you it's only a nomination but I feel you have a great chance.'

'Umm glass conservatory in January?'

'Don't worry, it's centrally heated. It creates a wonderfully atmospheric venue in mid-winter,' he replied confidently having hosted this annual event for the past eight years.

25

The last letter to fall through the letterbox while Kate was still at her home was from Amal Zaidi. When she opened it she drew her breath in. The letter had a black surround. She sat down and read that Mr. Mohammad Zaidi died a week ago and in accord with Islamic rites, was buried two days later. It was a brief letter but one which required a more lengthy response. A tear fell from her eyes as she recalled Mr. Zaidi's friendship in so many ways.

Saturday came and the keys of the house were left under the doormat as agreed by the Estate Agents. Kate took up residence with Bruce at his family home which was a self-contained stone building – a former manse with a glebe attached.

It was there where Kate replied to Amal in a letter of condolence together with a cheque for £250K and a much fuller explanation why the house was sold. She spoke of her sincere gratitude for the house which launched her career with her mobile hairdressing and now, managing director of Seaweed in My Hair. Finally, she urged Amal to stay with them in summer if not before.

Christmas came and went with little celebration. On Hogmanay Bruce proposed that on 1st March, they would be married at the registrar's office in Brodick. There would be a reception afterwards at The Douglas Hotel.

On 19th January, just before the start of the Burns Supper season got underway, Lizzie with Alan came up from London, Amal stayed with Kate and Bruce in the old manse and the good and great of Arran were in attendance when they met to deliver the community awards.

Jack Smith took the young athlete's award having been selected to run for the Scottish under 18s. There were two other runners up, who received book tokens.

The Community Awards were better contested. From Lochranza came Grandparents for Reading. A library event held twice a week where Grandparents read to children and encouraged them to read, outside school hours.

From Lamlash, the Girl Guides who had formed a beach clean-up throughout the year. From Corrie, a boy who had become a young accordionist playing to senior citizens in care homes regularly. And finally, from Kildonan a girl of four who had telephoned for an ambulance when she saw a woman collapse in the street outside her home. It was a difficult choice but Chairman for the evening Hugh Boag informed those present that a tie had been declared. The two winners were Ann McNeil from Kildonan and Fraser Knowles from Corrie.

Neither young child was present but their respective parents accepted their awards on their behalf.

Finally came the Business Person of the Year Award. Bruce patted Kate's knee under the table. 'Good luck, darling.'

Hugh stood up to reveal the contenders of the final category. 'Again, not an easy one to judge. We have whittled the nominations down to three. Mavis Barker of Lamlash for her patchwork quilts sewn and sent to Bangladesh; Senya Mensah from Brodick for her popular beads artwork and finally Kate Bailey for her Seaweed in My Hair products taken on by the chemists Boots, employing several people on the island of Arran and the UK. And our winner is...Kate Bailey.'

'Well done darling. Up you go and collect your award.'

'Perhaps you'd like to say a few words Kate,' whispered Hugh into her ear.

Kate stepped forward having received the silver trophy. 'This is quite overwhelming. Firstly, because I've never, ever won an award in my life before,' she said and a sympathetic laugh was heard around the glass conservatory. 'Secondly, I'm really just a newcomer, still finding my feet on the most beautiful island I could have imagined. And finally, some people have made this award possible. I'm pleased they are all here to hear me say this, without the financial and loving support from Amal Zaidi, an Arran lover known to many of you, this project would not have taken off the ground. And how could I forget another true supporter who saw the potential in me, the man I recently became engaged to and the man I'll marry in two months time, the author Bruce Butler.' She stopped to look at him and some seated left their seats to applaud which in turn caused all to stand and continue applauding. Whether they were applauding our engagement and announcement to marry, about the jobs the project had created or that it was the final award, Kate did not know. She returned to her seat amid back slapping and applause at her table where Bruce met her and kissed her cheek.

'Well done darling. Your award is well earned.'

26

The silver cup award stood on the mantelpiece in the lounge. Over the years further awards would come Kate's way, many in the form of a cheque.

On 1st March at the Brodick registrar's room, in the presence of only Amal, Lizzie, and Alan, Bruce betrothed his love to Kate and she responded likewise. Kate was glad to let go of her surname Bailey, those memories were fast leaving her memory.

The reception seemed to have invited everyone from Blackwaterfoot. Hugh had ensured the Annan Banner photographer was present to record the occasion and Bruce wondered which of the many flashes in his eyes would be in the paper. Marge Orr, Kate's former neighbour, turned out to be a mover and shaker around the dance floor and Mrs. McSkimming drummed her fingers on the table to the ceilidh band in full swing.

All seemed to have enjoyed a wonderful evening in the hotel that night.

The following day, a letter arrived which had Kate's old address. She opened it. It was from Greg.

'Congratulations on your marriage. I wish you well. I am living with Patricia now. We are getting along just fine. Thanks for those seven happy years. Best wishes Greg.' Kate smiled. She did not care whether he knew she was on Arran or not. She had a new life. However, she was touched that he had written to her and as Mrs. Butler, she replied to him in a similar vein a few days later.

On November 22nd the following year, Kate gave birth to twins, both were boys and identical. It wasn't long before Kate brought out her scissors to cut their hair. They had baby shampoo. Bruce on the other hand washed his hair with Seaweed in My Hair. There were stocks of the shampoo in the cupboards and the toothpaste of the same name sat in a cup by the sink. And in the kitchen cupboard some Seaweed in My Hair energy bars.

And this story ends in a very traditional manner. Yes, it's true. They lived happily ever after.

The End

ACKNOWLEDGEMENTS

This is my opportunity to express my gratitude to so many in so many different ways who have helped me complete this trilogy of Arran stories. Or is it the Arran Noir trilogy or perhaps better remembered as my Covid 19 Lockdown Trilogy? Grateful thanks go to Police Scotland for their help in the finer details of each story. Others I dare not forget to mention can now take a bow; Morag Ritchie, Alan Collins, Alan Nicolson, Margaret Nicolson, Stuart, and Joyce Bell. To Mandy J Steel Collins for her support, patience, and all the other tasks undertaken by this superb editor and publisher at Beul Aithris Publishing. Finally to Jocelyn, my wife, who lets me hog the computer providing I make soup but she always gives me time to dream, plot, and plan as I start a new page. And extra finally to Georgie, okay walkies now.

Interview With The Author

Blackwaterfoot is a village. Why set another east coast Arran thriller here?

If you have read *Murders at Blackwaterfoot* and *Dementia Adventure* you will realise I have a love for the village and the island. There's something mystic about the east coast of Arran; its caves, the mist, the hamlets of honest people. It's the entire opposite of Fulham or Chelsea where Kate and Greg came from. No wonder they wanted a change and change is what this story is about.

What do you know about hairdressers or physical fitness instructors?

On the former, I have a wife and two daughters. I rest my case and clear the trapped hair from the bath. It ain't mine, of course. My fitness regime, for me, is with the over 70's badminton players and on dog walks. And where would I be without the internet! The great jazz musician Duke Ellington was once asked how he could play so well without a musical education. He replied; a beaver don't go to engineering school to build a dam. Likewise, I write about what I know and not what I do.

Do you make a plan of your story before writing it?

No. I plan the first page and then let the story flow. Ideas are always on my mind. It's the way I work. It makes the editing arduous but worthwhile.

Will you retire to Arran?

I know I should retire to Arran. It has been a family holiday venue for many years over three or four generations. It seems like a natural home. But it has almost always been a summer or autumn visit. What would seal it for me would be if both daughters as a procurator fiscal and a clinical psychologist found work on Arran, we'd be settled on the island in an instant. Where? Blackwaterfoot of course.

What is your next book?

The Dream Net is heading towards its conclusion. More details after Dementia Adventure.

What is a Jane Austin Literary Mentor?

Since 2019 I have been working as a Jane Austin Literary mentor, supporting evolving children writers all over the world. A writing career offers many opportunities. I am delighted to be working with children from Saudi Arabia and Qatar so far. I will be reading what Ghanaian children have written soon. It is immensely satisfying to encourage youngsters all over the world, to take a first step with a pencil or pen. Being able to nourish a writer in the making, is an honour.

Other Books By Miller Caldwell

Novels

Operation Oboe
The Last Shepherd
Restless Waves
Miss Martha Douglas
The Parrot's Tale
Betrayed in the Nith
The Crazy Psychologist
The Trials of Sally Dunning
A Clerical Murder
A Lingering Crime *
A Reluctant Spy **
Caught in a Cold War Trap **

*This book is in the hands of New York film director Daniel Guardino.

**Denotes books on 'Optioned' status with French film company ARTE.

Biographies

Untied Laces
Jim's Retiring Collection
Poet's Progeny
7 point 7 on the Richter Scale
Take the Lead
Children's books

Chaz the Friendly Crocodile
Lawrence the Lion Seeks Work
Danny the Spotless Dalmatian

Self-Help

Have You Seen My Ummm... Memory?
Ponderings IN LARGE PRINT
It's Me, Honest It Is

Coming soon

A Dream Net

Printed in Great Britain
by Amazon

65460816R00177